THE WEDDING

A NEW JOURNEY - BOOK 2

THE WEDDING

A NEW JOURNEY - BOOK 2

SAMANTHA KANNAN

ACKNOWLEDGEMENTS

This book wouldn't be possible if it weren't for several people. The first is my husband, Kannan, who always believed in me and supported my dreams. I'm also very thankful for his family who accepted me and helped me in every step along the way, especially his sister Subha. I'd like to thank my friend Jurnee Clark for giving me permission to use her name, and Mellissa Roemer, Krista Bronnenberg, and Bridget Winitzer for helping me with my preliminary edits. Devi Annamalai, Dr. Vasanthan Thirunavukkarasu, Sharlie Thiyagarajan, Priyan Raj, Sethurama Iyer, and Narendran Sundhara Rajan were endlessly helpful in making sure that my accounts were accurate and nothing was misrepresented. And for double checking everything again, I'd like to thank Amber Gill, Mara Nestark, and Naushard Cader. Without Mystique Roberts, I never been able to start writing, and Jenna Moreci's YouTube videos provided endless insights into the writing process. Professionally, I'd like to thank Jegannath Ramanujam for bringing my vision for the cover to life [jegananimation.wixsite.com/creativehands], Caroline Barnhill for her patience and encouragement with editing [fiverr.com], and Kari Holloway for her beautiful formatting [khformatting.com]. It would be a crime to not mention some of my biggest encouragers— the friends I've made online through Quora, Twitter, Instagram, and TikTok. I'm forever thankful for your kindness and support, and I hope you enjoy reading my book.

CHAPTER 1

The final bell rang as I bid a Friday farewell to my students. *My* students. It was still surreal that I finally had my own class. I finally had my own students. I had a job. I had Anooj, too. Life was perfect.

As I walked to my car, I checked my phone. Surely he had slept by now as it was about 2 a.m. in India. Long-distance relationships were just as tough as they said in all the forums I had read online, the primary difficulty being a nearly twelve-hour time difference. Our days were mismatched and, with opposite work and sleeping schedules, the few hours a day we had that intersected were precious.

Good morning, I texted him. He wouldn't get it for a few hours, but it was our daily ritual. I texted him after school got out, he called me when he woke up. We had settled into a good rhythm over the past six months since meeting in India where I had taught English in the southern state of Kerala.

It was stressful being apart, but it was necessary for now. I was busy preparing for my new job all summer, busy teaching in the fall and spring, it was too cold for him in the winter. Hopefully he could come in the summer, and, maybe, I'd be able to go to India again during winter holidays. It was September, so I had to decide soon if I was going. It felt like ages since we had seen each other.

It wasn't just Anooj that I missed. I missed the school. The students. Joseph. My colleagues. Mellissa. It had been so tough leaving everyone. The only thing was that Anooj was no longer in Trivandrum, so it would be more difficult to visit him and the school since his family had moved back to Tamil Nadu. It wasn't too far, but it would be difficult.

I had tried to stay in touch with everyone in Kerala. I'd gotten friend requests from most everyone on Facebook, and some of them chatted with me on WhatsApp during school breaks. Even Mellissa and I were keeping in touch. I wasn't able to stay in touch with some of the teachers due to the language barrier and busy schedules in opposite time zones, but I still cared about them deeply.

Pulling into my driveway, I grabbed my school bag and went inside. One benefit of being a teacher was getting home a couple of hours before my parents so I could take a nap and be more awake at night to talk to Anooj.

I woke up and checked my phone. 7 p.m. Much later than I had wanted, but still too early for Anooj to be awake. I'd fallen in love with him these past few months, but living at opposite ends of the planet and opposite sides of the clock was hard.

With a quick splash of water on my face, I ran downstairs to find my parents watching old episodes of Jeopardy while they played Candy Crush. Yet ironically I was the one who they complained was on my phone all the time.

"Good morning, Sleeping Beauty," my father exclaimed.

"Ha. Ha," I said with a roll of my eyes.

"Any big parties tonight?" my mom asked sarcastically. They were full of jokes tonight. "What's for dinner?"

"I thought we'd order a pizza."

Yesss. Nothing was better than a Friday night pizza.

We ordered the usual from Domino's, but it reminded me of the Domino's in Kollam. Oddly, it had tasted so much better in India. It had been fresher, with so much more flavor. I literally had a dream about it over the summer. That would be among my first stops when I got back to India. Well, that and the biggest thinnest *dosa* that I could find with some *Mysore Pak*. The *Mysore Pak* I'd brought home was long gone. It had lasted just a couple of weeks between sharing with friends and family, and, of course, my own stomach. I found a box at the Indian grocery store, but nothing compared to the original melt-in-your-mouth crumbly goodness. I was homesick for a place that wasn't my home.

"So, what are your plans for the weekend, Jurnee?"

"I'm going out with Marina and Krista for lunch tomorrow, and I have a date with Anooj tomorrow night."

"Another dinner and a movie over Skype?"

We'd become predictable, but we had very limited options, being about ten thousand miles apart. We talked all the time, but since we couldn't go on dates, this was all we could do to feel closer. Being in a long-distance relationship was far from glamorous.

"Of course."

"When do we get to meet him?" My father had been bugging me about this for months, but I was nervous. I'd never been serious enough about someone to have them actually meet my parents, whether via Skype or in person. They noticed me blushing and looked at one another. They knew it was serious without me ever saying it outright.

I looked up gingerly, "Soon."

"Ok. Then how was school?"

"It's going really well! My students are doing great, and all the teachers are really helpful. Everything in third grade is perfect."

"We're glad to hear that, sweetie." They were equally relieved that my life had done a complete 180 since this time last year when I had struggled so much with being unable to find a job. I was at the top of my game. Finally.

The evening was spent in the same habit of watching whatever the latest thing on Netflix was and eating the same pizza. Some may see it as boring, but I really enjoyed this new mature relationship with my parents. It was like they were my roommates now, not my prison wardens.

Suddenly my phone rang, causing my parents to look at me in unison, "Anooj?"

I sheepishly looked down as I took my plate to the kitchen. "Tell him we said hi!" they shouted after me as I ran upstairs.

"Hello?" I answered as soon as I was out of earshot.

"Good morning, *Yathra*." What was meant as a one-time homage to my name back in India had escalated to being my new nickname.

"How did you sleep?" It still felt odd to ask him how his sleep had been when I knew that I would be sleeping very shortly.

"It was very good. You came in my dream."

"What happened in it?"

"We were walking around a fire."

"A fire? Was everything okay?"

"That is how our marriage ceremonies are here."

I couldn't help but to blush. Sure, I'd thought about it. Everything between us felt so natural. We had vastly different upbringings and experiences and religions, but our ideals and goals and personalities just blended so well. I'd never been able to talk to someone with as much ease as I was with him; he made me feel complete.

In a hushed tone, I asked, "Do you think we'll ever get married?"

"I know we will, Jurnee. I love you."

"I love you, too," I said softly.

"When will you tell me that you love me at full volume?" he asked jokingly.

"I know, I know." I felt bad, but I didn't want the same lectures from my parents that I'd been getting from my friends, especially Marina. She'd never even met him, but she'd disliked him from the moment she heard about him.

"Everything okay?"

"It is," I stammered. "I just- do people ever tell you that you're making a mistake by dating me?"

I could sense his voice change, "No. Did someone say that?"

"Some of my friends are just concerned. You know the stereotypes."

"You know I'm not like that, right? I'm perfectly happy here in India, and I'd love to settle here. It's entirely your wish."

"I know. And honestly, I'd love to live in Kerala forever."

"Jurnee, we're back in Tamil Nadu now remember."

"Oops." I kept forgetting.

"*Paravaala*," he said nonchalantly. He'd been trying to teach me basic Tamil for a couple of months. I knew that this one basically meant *no problem.* "When you do you want to come see Tamil Nadu?"

"I'm going to try to come over Christmas break. But next summer you definitely have to come here, okay? I want to introduce you to everyone so they can see for themselves how great you are."

"I am pretty great, aren't I?" he joked. But he really was great, I'd never met anyone like him.

I wished so desperately that we could, at the very least, live in the same hemisphere. We were at exact opposite ends of the earth, and it was much more difficult than I had anticipated.

"I really miss you, Anooj. Do you want to switch to video?"

"Wait, let me make myself beautiful for you," he said with a laugh as I heard the faucet turning on in the background. "Just have to quickly wash my face."

The familiar beep on WhatsApp notifying me that the other party wished to convert our call from audio to video suddenly chirped. He looked the same as he did every night when I called him. His shaggy black hair was messy from sleep, eyes barely open, but smiling from ear to ear.

How did I get so lucky? I thought to myself. He was the perfect person, just a few thousand miles too far.

"I really miss you, Jurnee. Every day that I am without you feels like it has been wasted."

"I miss you, too." I was so happy to see him, but I felt an inexplicable sadness. Every time we had a video call, it was obvious how far we were. He had just woken up; the sun was shining through his window. It almost made me feel like we were further apart than closer together.

"Then how was school? Tell me everything about the day."

He knew that the best way to stop my ever-present inner monologue was to make me talk. It was uncanny how well he knew me and understood me. We continued talking for hours before I finally fell asleep in the call.

When I woke up, it was 11 a.m., and I was nearly late for meeting Marina and Krista, two of my best friends from college. I briefly resented them when they had found teaching jobs before me, but I knew that my time would eventually come. And it did.

I wore my weekend uniform of jeans and a fitted T-shirt, and made sure to grab my flipflops before the autumn air got too cold for them. Pulling my hair back into a clip for a lazy half-ponytail, I grabbed my phone, keys, and wallet in one swoop and headed downstairs.

"Be back in a bit!" I shouted to whoever was listening. I didn't have to ask permission anymore. I didn't have to tell them precisely what time I would be back. I didn't have to give them my friends' numbers. My life had truly changed since I started working; I had become an adult.

I was always the first one to arrive to anything. A meeting, event, lunch with friends. It was always me who requested the table. When the restaurant hostess turned to me, I knew the script already without them needing to ask, "Three for Jurnee," I said as I saw her write Bernie. It wasn't the first time.

As I sat on the bench, I could see Marina's car pulling up. We were like clockwork. I was the early one, Marina came right on the dot of the meeting time, and Krista would come eventually. The hostess was now long familiar with "Bernie" and the gang, so she led us to our seats early.

We had barely sat down before Marina launched into her latest gossip. "Oh. My. God. Did you hear about Karen?"

Karen was a girl who had graduated a year before us in college. "No, what happened?"

"She had married that foreign guy she met in school, remember?"

"Oh, yeah. Their wedding last summer was so beautiful."

"Until he left her."

"Wait. What?" They had seemed so happy together. I wondered what could have happened in just a year.

"Jenny said that Alex said that she heard that he left suddenly one day and had only been using her for a green card."

I felt so bad for Karen that I didn't even have words. She was one of the sweetest people I'd met during college. She was always so kind and helpful, and always had the best advice. "I hope she's okay. Should we call her?"

"Call who?" Krista asked as she reached the table.

"Karen," Marina started. "Her husband left her. The foreign one."

"She only had one husband, Marina. You don't need to differentiate." Krista always knew how to shut down the gossip train. That was one thing I loved about her.

Marina rolled her eyes as Krista sat down and opened her menu. "So, what are we having?"

We didn't order the usual way anymore. We now ordered three meals and split them equally rather than being confined to a single dish. Anooj had taught me this trick in India, and everyone loved it. Well, except for my mom. She was very territorial about her food.

"Jurnee. Earth to Jurnee," Marina said with a snap in front of my face. "What are we having?"

"I'll get the Cajun Shrimp Pasta vegetarian."

"I thought you'd grow out of your vegetarian phase after college. Why are you still like this? It's so hard to share with you."

"I feel so bad for them. Just raised to die. My life isn't so important that someone else should sacrifice theirs for me for a single meal."

"Jurnee. I love you. That's why I care. But you need to chill. You have thumbs. Your life has more value."

It was my turn to roll my eyes. Marina had good intentions, she was just very blunt.

"What you're doing is noble, Jurnee. Don't listen to her," Krista chipped in.

"I don't do it to be noble. I just feel guilty," I said with a shrug.

"Okay, then. But we haven't decided what we're all getting. So Jurnee is getting the Cajun Shrimp Pasta vegetarian. Krista?"

It took a while, but we eventually settled on what to order for the table just as the waitress came over. Marina, of course, ordered for us. She was like our gossipy mom. She was strong, knew what she wanted, and always told it like it was. In some ways, I wished I could be more like her. Krista was also strong, but much more gentle.

"So Jurnee, are you still liking everything at St. Joseph's?"

"I absolutely love it."

"And you're sure you're okay with staying with your parents? You're always welcome to stay at my apartment. I could use a roommate."

"That's okay. I'm saving up money to move out next summer. I actually kind of like staying with them."

"Wait," Marina interjected. "Are you serious?"

"Yeah. Our relationship is so much better now that I'm more independent. It's like we're friends now."

"And what about *Anooj*?" Marina said with a slight lilt.

"Things are going great. We're having another Skype date tonight."

"Jurnee. You could get any guy here. Why are you settling for some random guy in India of all places? You could easily have him," she said gesturing to a random guy at a nearby table. "Or him," she pointed to another. "Probably even him," she pointed.

Luckily Krista was there to back me up. "She's happy, Marina. Just let her be."

"I don't want her to get scammed like Karen, okay. He could be using her for a green card. Say everything sweet and nice to her now and run away as soon as he gets it."

"He wouldn't do that."

"Have you *met* him?"

Krista stammered, "Well... no... but I trust Jurnee's judgement."

I looked to Krista with a silent thank you passing from my eyes to hers.

"Jurnee. I love you. You know that," Marina said softly. "I'm just worried about you. Do you really know him that well? What if he's a criminal or planning to keep you in a harem or sell your kidneys? There are worse things than just using someone for a green card."

Despite now looking at the floor, I could feel Krista's disapproving glare radiating towards Marina. She had stepped too far this time. "I'll just go use the ladies' room," I announced to the table, still looking at the floor. I had never been so happy than I'd been with Anooj, but it was so hard when we were so far apart and the opposition was so strong.

As soon as I reached the bathroom, I could feel the warmth from behind my eyes releasing itself as I cried over the sink. *You have one minute to wallow, then it's back outside,* I told myself sternly.

I felt my heart sink as Marina walked into the bathroom. This was humiliating. "Jurnee," she said as a tear rolled down her cheek. "I'm sorry. I just care so much about you and I'm so worried. Are you sure he's right for you?"

"I'm positive," I said as she wrapped her arms around me. Just then Krista came in as well, and the three of us made quite the scene hugging in the bathroom while two of us cried.

"Okay. From now on, I'm totally supportive. No more negative talk."

I breathed a sigh of relief. Being in a long-distance relationship was hard enough on its own, but when someone is against it, it gets so much harder. I wasn't sure if Marina's resolution would stick, but I was hopeful. At least my parents, Krista, and most others were supportive.

"We love you, Jurnee. And we're so glad that you're happy," Krista piped in as she squeezed both of us a little tighter.

Our food was cold by the time we made it back into the dining room, but luckily the tension had cooled off, too.

When I got back home, I just needed a nap. I was glad that we were all mostly on the same page now, but it had been draining.

"How was lunch?" my mom called as I went upstairs.

"Good! Taking a nap now!" I shouted down. These afternoon naps were really helpful in letting me stay up later to spend time with Anooj. Or did I just really need them since I was staying up so late every day? It was a bit of a chicken and the egg conundrum.

Settling down into bed, I checked my phone once.

It was Marina. *Jurnee, I'm so sorry. I know you may still be upset, but I'm just worried about you. I love you and don't want you to be hurt.*

I know, I replied. *I love you too.*

Krista had sent one too. *Sorry about earlier. Marina and I had a long talk, and we wholly support you and Anooj. Can't wait to meet him!* That was a relief.

I didn't know what else to say, so I just sent a smiling emoji to each and checked to be sure my phone was on silent before nodding off.

A couple of hours later, I woke up groggy. Naps were always a gamble. Sometimes I would wake up feeling like I'd slept for twelve hours and ready conquer the world, other times I was barely able to open my eyes. Today it was somewhere in between, but closer to the side of barely able to open my eyes.

The first thing I always did was check my phone. Was it late enough for Anooj to be awake? Nope, only 5. No missed messages yet either, so I decided to go through my lesson plans for the coming week and make sure that everything was in order.

My students were doing well with their coursework. I'd only known them for a month, but they were flying through my material. Their families were so sweet and welcoming when they found out that I was a first-year teacher. The kids themselves were so well-behaved, and it almost felt too perfect. It wasn't possible for life to align this easily.

Having gone through most of the material during my planning period in the previous week, I finished up everything in no time and checked my phone again. Still only 6. I wondered if Anooj also waited for me to wake up like this. We didn't really get a chance to talk in American morning time since I had to rush to school, so this was the only time we could really talk. I decided to go downstairs.

"Jurnee! How has your day been?" My dad was always so excited when I came down to chat. I made a note to do it more often. I went from being busy with school to being busy feeling sorry for myself, to being busy working and busy with Anooj. I didn't really give them much time anymore.

"Going well. Lunch with Marina and Krista, went over my lesson plans for next week, dinner with Anooj later."

"How *is* Anooj doing?"

He had a weird inflection. What did the inflection mean? "He's doing well."

"Is he planning a trip here anytime soon?" It felt repetitive to be asked the same questions almost daily, but I knew he was just excited to get to know Anooj.

"I don't know. We're thinking about him coming next summer for a little bit."

"Great! Any chance your mother and I could talk to him sometime before that?"

I didn't have a problem with it, but I didn't want them to be weird and ruin things. "Why?"

"No reason. You're both getting pretty serious though, aren't you? Six months is a long time. We just want to get to know him."

I *really* didn't want them to ruin things with Anooj. And equally, I didn't want my parents to go off on a Marina-style tangent about how I was naïve and potentially ruining my life. I liked things how they were and really didn't want anything to change. "Sure. I'll talk to him," I said, against my better judgement.

We sat in comfortable silence. That was one of my favorite things about my dad. We didn't necessarily have to be talking or doing anything to spend time together. He didn't pry or try to boss me around, but he was always there when I needed him. I leaned my head on his shoulder as we continued watching *The Office* for the twelve-thousandth time. It was a reliable favorite.

"Where's Mom?" I asked after we had finished a couple of episodes.

"She was inspired by your lunch today and organized her own little girls' night."

"Won't you be lonely then with her out and me with Anooj?"

He smiled peacefully, "I knew this would happen when you started growing up. I'm just happy that we get to see you every day still."

"Me too," I said as I gave him a big hug. "I love you, Dad."

"I love you too, sweet pea."

Before I knew it, my phone started vibrating.

"Anooj, huh?"

"Yep," I futilely tried to contain my smile, but it could not be contained.

"Say hi to him from us."

I smiled with a confirming nod as I answered the call and ran upstairs.

"Hello?"

"Good morning, *Yaathra*. How was the day?"

"It was good, how was your sleep?"

"Quite lonely. You were not there today."

"Got busy, sorry," I teased.

"How was lunch with your friends?"

I didn't want to get into it. "It was okay."

"*Ennachu?*" More Tamil practice. This one meant *what happened* if I recalled correctly.

"Nothing happened. It's just that not everyone totally understands our relationship."

"What did they say?"

"The usual. What if you're using me for a green card? What if you're just using me until you get an arranged marriage? What if you're trying to sell me into an organ trafficking ring?"

"You know that I only love your kidneys inside of you, right? They won't have the same charm if they're extracted."

I couldn't help but to laugh. He had the most bizarre sense of humor. "I really wish you were here," I said quietly.

"Let's not watch a movie tonight," he suggested.

"Why, what happened? I thought we were set to see *Premam* again tonight?"

"I can't take much more of this love triangle between us and Nivin Pauly. I'm beginning to get jealous."

I audibly laughed. It was true, I did have a major crush on Nivin, the lead actor in *Premam* and the most handsome actor in all Malayalam cinema, but no way would anything come of it. Firstly, he was famous. Secondly, he was married with a child. Thirdly, I was in a serious relationship. It just wasn't in the cards for us. "Fiiine. Then what do you want to see?"

"Let's just talk. I like to hear your voice."

"This voice?" I said with a bit of grit.

"Very funny," he said as the notification rang through to change the call to video.

He liked to dress up for our "dates." Tonight it was a light blue button up shirt and his hair combed to the side, oily like an accountant. I was just wearing a simple black sweater with a white Peter Pan collar and my wavy hair hanging loose down my back.

"You always look so beautiful, Jurnee."

"Anooj?"

"What is it?"

"I don't want to be apart anymore."

"We'll meet soon, don't worry. It's just a few months away, and then you won't be able to get rid of me."

"But then we'll be apart again after that."

"But, Jurnee, one day we'll never be apart, and then you will be wishing for these peaceful days again."

I laughed again. He always had this way of making me feel at ease. Even when I was extremely tense, he just knew exactly what to say to shake me out of it. "Do you really think we'll be together always, even despite our differences?"

"Our differences are only our circumstance by birth. Our nationality, religion, skin color – none of these are chosen items. I love the person behind your labels."

"How did you get to be so perfect?"

"I should ask you the same thing."

I could feel the heat radiating from my cheeks as I looked down and couldn't help but to laugh.

"So shy, Jurnee. No wonder they said you have the heart of a Malayali. Are you sure that you're American?"

It sometimes bothered me, all the stereotypes that I heard against Americans – how we were loud or dumb or drunkards or lacking morals. People would say these to me as if it was a compliment, but I felt a bit odd. I knew that they meant the best, so I tried not to dwell on it, but I still didn't like it. "I *am* an American. Why do you need to insult someone else to give a small compliment to me?"

He paused. Did I say too much?

"You're right," he said. "I didn't mean it badly; I should think more how I phrase things."

In six months, we had never fought. I was certain that the majority of that had to do with being in a long-distance relationship. But, more than that, another part was how maturely he handled everything. He was slow to react, willing to admit when he made a mistake, always honest even when it was negative, never tried to pass a blame onto anyone else. And, best of all, he didn't just say things to say them. When he said he would do something, he *meant* it. Every day, he inspired me to be a better person. I could trust him with anything.

"I know, Anooj. So, what do you want to do when I go there?"

"We're in Madurai now, so I can show you Meenakshi Temple or we can have *jigarthanda* or I can show you some museums. We have a Domino's, too."

"What if I only see you?" What was *jigarthanda*?

"I am boring. We'll see the city also."

"And I can meet your family and friends, too! My parents want to meet you soon, too."

He hesitated. I wondered what I said that was wrong.

"Anooj?"

"When shall I meet them?"

"I don't know. They're curious who this boy is that I am always talking to."

"I can meet them now. Are they still awake? Call them."

"Now? Are you sure?"

"I'm dressed properly and my hair is combed, now is the best time."

I chuckled with a shrug as I went downstairs. "Mom! Dad!" I shouted from the stairs, unsure if my mom was home yet.

Sitting on the couch watching TV, they looked up worriedly. "What happened?"

"Anooj wants to meet you."

My mom's face instantly lit up as she looked at my father and stood. She was almost giddy as they made their way to the stairs, and, for a moment, I regretted my choice. What if they hated each other? What if this ruined our relationship?

They raced up the stairs as I led the way to my room. Open on my desk was Anooj looking like he was in an interview via Skype. "Hi, Mr. and Mrs. Ryan. I am Anooj, nice to meet you."

CHAPTER 2

I t's so nice to meet you, Anooj! You can call me Vanessa, no need to be so formal."

"Ok, Vanessa Auntie." I had forgotten about the *auntie* thing and was worried for a moment, but my mom seemed to think that it was cute, so I didn't dwell on it. It was so nerve-wracking to observe them. Everything seemed to be going well, but I was still worried.

I tried to distract myself by going through my phone, but then I slowly began pacing. I decided to go downstairs and have some water, then come back.

But it made me more nervous to be away from the call. How were they doing? Did everyone like each other? What were they talking about? What if my parents said something embarrassing about me? What if Anooj said something embarrassing about me? No. No. No. I ran upstairs.

As worried as I had been, it all melted away instantly. They were all laughing. I could have sworn that I heard my dad call him *son*. Was it really that easy to introduce a boy to your parents? I'd never done it before and had been expecting the worst, especially after Marina's little show this afternoon.

"Oh honey, you're back!" my mom exclaimed as she noticed me walk in. "Anooj is an absolute delight!"

My dad saved the day, though. "We won't compromise your date any longer, you kids have fun," he said as he closed the door.

And with that, it was over. My parents had met Anooj, and they loved him. It couldn't have gone better.

Sitting down, I looked to Anooj. "Soooooo?"

"I cannot tell you anything, I've been sworn to secrecy," he teased.

"No, you haven't. Tell me everything now."

"You shouldn't have left me alone then."

He was right, but I was still curious.

"Okay, okay, fine. They just asked the basic auntie uncle questions. What do you do? How is your family? Normal stuff only. But much less intense than an interrogation here would be."

"What do you mean?"

"Here they will ask your salary, when you plan to marry, what your marks were, your astrology details, everything."

"Oh, no. Is this what I should be expecting when I meet your mom?" His father had passed a few years prior.

"She'll be gentle. Don't worry."

"When will I meet her?"

"After some time."

"Why not now? Call her here. You just met my parents."

"It isn't that simple, Jurnee."

Why was he suddenly being weird? Was he hiding her from me? Or was he hiding me from her? "It is that simple."

"Jurnee, I-"

"My parents love you. I should meet your mom also."

"Jurnee, you cannot yet meet her."

"Why?"

"Well, I," he paused. "The thing is that... Jurnee, she doesn't yet know about you."

I was in shock. Just a moment ago everything was perfect. He was meeting my parents, everyone was laughing, our future seemed so clear and perfect. And now, suddenly, it had just melted away in the blink of an eye. I didn't say anything. I couldn't get any words out. I just stared at him. I had always just assumed that she knew about me the same way my parents knew about him.

Maybe I was being dramatic. Okay, definitely being dramatic. But I felt betrayed. Like everything had been an illusion.

"Jurnee, things are not so simple here."

"It's been *six* months, Anooj. How could your family possibly not know about me? Who do they think you're in calls with every day?"

"You have been to India. You know things are different here."

"So, all that that you said about our wedding and our future and everything, it wasn't real. You were just saying it." How could he keep me a secret like this?

"I meant it. It is just difficult to tell them right now."

"What could possibly be difficult to tell them? You said it wasn't an issue with your friends, then what's the problem with your family?"

"Jurnee, I am the only son. She has been dreaming of arranging my marriage since I was born."

Without warning or prompting, tears fell from my eyes like a sudden rainfall on a sunny day. "So, you're getting an arranged marriage?" Had Marina been right?

"I didn't say that, Jurnee. I said that *she* has been dreaming of it. I have not been. But I need time to tell this to her in a way that she will accept."

"What's so bad about me?"

"Nothing is bad about you, there are just some complications."

"Like what?"

"Jurnee-," he started, but I cut him off. How could he do this to me?

"Like. What?"

"Ok," he said as he took a deep breath. "Firstly, you're American."

"So what if I'm American? There are so many Indian people who are American. Germans who are American. Ethiopians who are Americans. What does my passport have to do with anything?"

"There are some stereotypes about white Americans that we will have to work to overcome."

"What stereotypes?"

"You remember everything people at school said to you. They said you don't seem at all like an American. Remember that?"

"So?"

"So, we have certain ideas about Americans that may be difficult for my family to move past."

"Everyone at school moved past it, they can, too. I can get letters of recommendation from them just like I had for my interviews."

"I know, Jurnee, it is just a complication. I didn't say that this won't work, just that we need to be strategic about how I tell everyone when the time comes."

"Then what else?"

"You're Christian."

"So?"

"Christians often come here to do conversions. My family doesn't really like Christians because of this."

"Then I won't convert them. Next."

"It isn't that simple, Jurnee. This is much more complicated than you realize."

"Then why did you even tell me that you liked me to begin with?"

"Because I do, Jurnee. I love you. And we *will* end up together, we just have to approach it differently with my family than with your family."

"Then what else? My nationality and my religion apparently go against me."

"You don't know Tamil," he added hesitantly.

"So?"

"How will you communicate effectively with my family? With my extended family? How can our kids get a good grasp of Tamil if their mother doesn't know it?"

My first instinct was a rush of joy that he had seen so far into our future together and imagined our children, but it was immediately washed away by the rest. He had thought everything out very clearly, without involving me at all. He let me go on for months thinking that everything was perfect when there were so many complications lurking beneath the surface. How dare he? "It can't be that hard. I'll learn. What else?"

"That's mostly everything."

"Okay, so my nationality, religion, and language. Basically everything about me is wrong. Great." Everything that he said didn't matter, mattered. My labels that he said didn't mean anything meant everything.

"Not like that. You're perfect."

"Clearly I'm not."

"One other thing," he started.

Great. What more could there possibly be?

"Well, see. We don't really believe in dating, so I can't tell them until we are absolutely ready to get married."

"So, I have to be a secret girlfriend until then?"

"Jur-"

"A secret girlfriend like I'm twelve years old."

"Not like that."

"Then what like? Does this not seem extremely juvenile to you? Hiding one of the biggest aspects of your life from the people who literally created you and who care about you more than anyone else? Seriously?" I had gone from sad, to devastated, to hopeful, to furious.

"Jurnee, I'm sorry."

I didn't even want to hear it. He was ashamed of me. Maybe he had a hundred more secret girlfriends. Maybe he had been playing me this whole time while I was telling everyone I'd ever met what an amazing person I was dating. For a brief moment I wondered if I had overreacted, but I felt betrayed.

"I'm going to sleep, bye," I said without giving him a chance to reply. I promptly shut my laptop and turned out the light. When I looked at the phone, I realized that it was only 8:30. I hadn't yet eaten, but I didn't feel like it anymore. All dressed up, I covered myself in blankets as I turned off my phone and cried myself to sleep. This was our first fight, and it was horrible.

I woke up to one of the worst headaches of my life. Curious about the time, I turned on my phone to find twenty-seven missed calls. Tons of messages. Not just WhatsApp. He'd messaged me on Facebook, Instagram, Twitter, even email.

They were mostly apologies. Asking me to call him back. Saying that he would tell his family if it was that important to me. The phone started ringing. Anooj.

I let it ring three times as I debated on whether or not to answer. "Hello?"

"Jurnee, I'm so sorry, okay? I'll tell them. I'll tell them everything."

"I understand, Anooj. You must have had a good reason if you wanted to keep me a secret from the entire world," I said sarcastically, having just had my entire universe shattered.

"I don't *want* to, Jurnee. That's just how it is here. We aren't open like Americans."

I didn't know what to say. In all honesty, I didn't really want to say anything anyway.

"Jurnee, I love you. Please don't be angry on me."

I couldn't just turn it off though. It was stuck in the back of my mind. He didn't think I was good enough. Everything that he was for me, I wasn't for him. My family loved him, but his family didn't even know that I existed. "I have to go, Anooj."

"Go where? Jurnee, please listen to me."

"I can't right now," I said as I cut the call. My heart was broken. Just yesterday I saw our future being painted in the stars, but it was so easily washed away.

I tried to watch *The Office.* I tried to absentmindedly scroll through Facebook. I couldn't possibly talk to my parents about this. Marina was absolutely out of the question. I called Krista.

"Hello?" she answered on the first ring.

"Krista?"

She could probably hear the tears in my voice. "Are you home? I'm coming right now. I'll bring you some donuts."

I couldn't help but to start crying again. She knew me so well.

Within twenty minutes, she was in my bed.

"Jurnee, what happened?" she asked worriedly as she passed the box of donuts to me.

"Anooj," I could barely say his name. "I think we broke up."

"What? Why! You both seemed so happy."

"He met my parents last night."

"Did it not go well?"

"No, it went great. They all love each other, and it was so promising. They were even laughing."

"Then what happened?"

"He hasn't told his parents about me."

"Well that's alright. It's only been a few months."

"Six months, Krista. Six months."

"Did he say why?"

"He said that in India they don't tell their parents that they are dating someone until they're ready to get married, and it will be a big problem because I'm American and Christian and don't know their language. And, apparently, they've been dreaming of arranging his marriage since he was born. But, like, if he knew he had to get an arranged marriage then why would he even start dating me? He was the one who said he liked me first. Did he even think for five seconds before doing so?"

Tears silently dripped from my face as I took a big bite of donut and looked at her nervously, waiting for her to speak.

"You're absolutely right, and you know that I love you. You are an amazing person, and Anooj is so lucky to have you."

"He's amazing, too."

"Not right now, he isn't." I wanted to stand up for him, but I was too hurt to care at the moment. She took in my silence and continued, "But he may be right on some level."

Was she serious?

"Now, Jurnee. I love you, but hear me out."

I watched her intently as I furrowed my brow.

"This is India we're talking about. Not little old Indiana across the way. Things are so so different there. You saw it firsthand, right? All the stories you shared with us and the food, it's so different from here. It only makes sense for family dynamics to be different, too."

"But-"

"But nothing, Jurnee. Talk to him and listen more this time."

"But I don't want to listen."

"You love him, don't you?"

I looked down meekly; of course I did.

"See? You know that you do. Call him and patch this up."

I nodded in agreement. I knew she was right.

She hugged me as she got up, "I'll leave these with you," she said, gesturing to the donuts.

Starting on my second donut, my mom began knocking at the door. "Honey, is everything okay? Krista wasn't here very long."

The downside of living with your parents as an adult. "Yeah, everything is fine," I said not getting up from my bed. I didn't want to explain my puffy eyes to anyone.

"Are you sure?" she asked as she walked in.

"Mom! Privacy! I am twenty-three years old."

"A twenty-three-year-old with allergies!" she said as she ran to my side. "What *happened!*" she said as she pulled and prodded my eyelids, gaping at the swollen purple mess that used to be skin.

At least she didn't realize that I'd been crying all night. "Nothing happened. I'm fine."

"No, just wait here," she said as she ran downstairs. A minute later, she returned with water and Benadryl. "Take these and you'll be as good as new."

"Thanks, Mom."

"No problem at all. Tell Anooj we said hi," she said as she started towards the door.

"Will do."

"Did it go as well when you met his family, too?"

It was like someone pouring salt into my wound. I didn't know what else to do so I smiled and nodded. It wasn't technically lying, right?

She gave me that concerned mother look as she closed the door behind her.

Was I overreacting like Krista thought? It was weird that his family didn't even know that I existed, but I hadn't exactly dated anyone of a different cultural background before, so I hardly knew what was normal and what wasn't. I didn't *want* to be a secret girlfriend, but maybe that was normal there. After all, relationships are marathons, not sprints.

I looked down at my phone. Anooj had been calling me again, so I called him back. It only rang once.

"Hello?" he asked quickly.

"Anooj?"

"Jurnee, I'm sorry, okay? We can tell them. Everything will be fine, don't worry."

"No, it's okay. We'll wait."

"Jurnee, I love you more than anything. Things are just different here. Please give me more time."

"Okay." I resigned and decided to try it his way.

"When I come visit, everything will be easier. Please smile. I am doing this for us. When families become involved, everything becomes complicated."

"Especially when only one family is involved," I said under my breath. As much as I tried to move on from it, it did still bother me.

"What was that?"

"Why can't you just tell them, Anooj?" I broke down sobbing. Had I made this relationship out to be more than it actually was?

"Jurnee, one of two things would happen immediately after I tell them."

"And what are those?"

"If they like you, they will start planning our wedding right away. I know we love each other, but are we ready to get married right now?"

"Yes. Are you not?"

"That's not what I mean, Jurnee. It's just very complicated."

"Then what's the other possibility?"

He didn't answer.

"If they don't start planning our wedding, then what is the alternative?"

I could hear him drawing a deep breath. "We would have to break up."

"So, your family completely controls your life?"

"No, it's not like that. Jurnee, please see how tough this is."

What was there to see? He allegedly loved me, but he wouldn't even try to convince them if they disapproved.

"Even if your parents had disapproved, I wouldn't have continued with our relationship."

"That's how little I mean to you? You'll break up with me if anyone says no? Really?"

"It's not like that, Jurnee. We should respect our elders."

"And what about my respect? Why did you even say that you liked me if you knew that this was the outcome?"

"Because I see something in you."

"Clearly something that no one else sees. My nationality is wrong. My religion is wrong. My language is wrong. What else is there?"

"Your spirit, Jurnee. You're an amazing person, and I want to spend my life with you."

"Obviously not that badly," I said angrily. I had tried to move past it, but this was too much.

"Jurnee, I don't want to fight with you. Please try to understand."

"There's nothing to understand." I meant absolutely nothing to him, it was blatantly obvious.

"I love you, and I will explain it to them in time. Please trust me."

"Anooj," I said as tears streamed down my face. "I think we need to take a break."

"You don't mean that."

"I do. Until you can be sure that you want to be with me, I think this is for the best."

"For how long?"

"I don't know," I struggled to get out. I'd read before that heartbreak felt like someone was ripping your heart out of your chest. I always thought it was odd and melodramatic, but that was exactly what it felt like.

"Jurnee, don't do this."

"It's too late."

"If you want to take a break, then why not break up."

Now that invisible force was squeezing my heart, pressing its nails into it as they ripped it out. He couldn't be serious. I tried to get the words out, but they wouldn't come.

"Do you want to break up, Jurnee?" I could hear his voice breaking, but I couldn't get the words out. I wanted to stop him, but maybe he was right. Maybe this was for the best. Maybe we were too different.

"Fine. Let's break up," he said sternly as he cut the call. That was it. I had waited too long.

CHAPTER 3

I sat numb and fell backwards on the bed, staring at the ceiling. I couldn't feel anything. I couldn't even cry. I should call someone, but who? All I could do was look above me, eyes piercing through the ceiling. How did this escalate so fast? Was it my fault? It was Sunday afternoon. I had to be back at school in just a few hours.

Had I been too dramatic? Should I call him back? But I really didn't want to be a secret. I had more dignity than that. I laid staring at the ceiling as the sun quietly faded away. It took with it any hope that I had of getting back together.

A knock at the door. "Jurnee?" It was my mother. "Ready for dinner?"

"I'm not hungry!" I called weakly from the dark room under the blankets. I grabbed my phone for the first time in hours to see if he had texted me. I wasn't sure if I was more shocked that he hadn't texted me or that I had expected him to.

I looked around my empty room. We didn't even have a single photo together. Sure, we had some badly edited photos of us together. I caught myself chuckling for a moment before remembering that it was over. That there would be no more silly edited photos. That there would be no more future plans together. That it had all been temporary.

I thought back to my high school and college days. Sure, I'd had a short relationship before, but it hadn't taken hold of me as much as this one. It felt different. In the eight months that I'd known him, my entire life had woven around him.

The clock ticked beside me, almost taunting me. Counting the seconds since I'd been alone. We were up to eighteen thousand seconds. This was my life now. Without him.

I decided to watch *The Office* but got bored and turned it off. Something that had never happened before. I couldn't talk to any of my friends, because talking about this meant that I would have to relive it over and over again. It would mean that it had really happened.

I decided to watch *Premam* again. At the very least, Nivin Pauly could lift my spirits. But about halfway through, I realized that it was a huge mistake.

Watching George walk away from Malar's house with his friends after her accident devastated me in a way that it hadn't before. They had been so in love, and now she had amnesia. They were perfect together, but now it would never happen. I turned it off and reached to call Anooj again. I didn't want this to be us.

Below his name in WhatsApp, it said *Online*. When it changed to *Typing…*, my heart skipped a beat. After a minute, it went back to *Online*. I stared at his WhatsApp status until I fell asleep. I never received a message.

"Good morning, Jurnee!" My mom called as she knocked on my door. "Ready for breakfast?"

I most certainly was not. It felt like a truck had plowed into my head. Between my heart being broken, my eyes being swollen, and barely sleeping… I was not in a good state to teach a bunch of children. "What is it?" I called, sounding like an elderly frog with emphysema.

"Waffles!" she was much more chipper than normal and offering my favorite. She definitely knew something was up.

"Okay, I'll be down in a bit," I said as I wiped my eyes. It felt like tiny rock formations had grown around my eyes. Looking at my phone, I realized that I had slept through both alarms. Shit.

I picked a simple black midi dress with some midsized pearl earrings as I went to take a shower. It was so easy compared to my initial struggles with the showers I had used in Kerala. And would I ever use them again now that my strongest connection was now broken? I felt myself starting to cry again but stopped it. *You're late, Jurnee,* I scolded myself. *Pull yourself together. It's just a boy.*

Sitting through breakfast, I knew that my parents could tell that something was wrong. They didn't pry, though, for which I was very grateful.

At school, no one really noticed. A couple of my students said that I looked tired, but no one else said anything or acted any different. I wished that I hadn't been so open about our relationship in front of everyone. Maybe that was part of why Anooj didn't either. Maybe he didn't want to feel this constant nagging feeling of defeat and failure every time someone found out.

At lunch, I started and stopped at least a dozen messages to him. I thought about calling him. I couldn't bring myself to do it, though. My pride was masquerading as dignity. It had even fooled me.

Our Saturday brunch was the worst part of the entire breakup.

"Marina, Krista… I need to tell you something."

"What is it?" Marina asked.

"Is everything ok?" Krista sounded genuinely worried. She knew that Anooj and I had hit a rough patch, but she didn't know the full extent of it yet. I could already see the pity in her eyes, she knew what was coming.

"Anooj and I," I looked down. "We broke up."

Without a word, Marina and Krista wrapped me into their arms.

"You're better off without him anyway," Marina said. It wasn't true, though.

"Do you want to move this to my apartment?" Krista asked. She knew we needed the space, peace, and privacy to fully discuss what had happened.

I meagerly nodded my head as Marina left cash on the table and we walked out.

Krista's apartment was always immaculate. I had told her several times in college that it wasn't too late to change her major to interior design, but she had had her heart set on teaching art since she took her first art class back in elementary school.

I relayed it to them again. Blow by blow, I recounted how my life had gone from blissful perfection to utter destruction in just a few hours. It had been a week now, but it still felt like it had just happened.

"What did your parents say?" Krista asked.

"I haven't told them, but I'm pretty sure that they know something is up."

"Don't worry, Jurnee. We're here for you," Marina said as she squeezed our group hug. "You're better off anyway."

"Marina!" Krista spewed. "This is hardly the time."

"I'm just saying the truth."

Sometimes I didn't really like Marina, but even then, I always appreciated her for never being afraid to speak her mind.

"Do you think this is it, or will you patch things up? Have you talked since?"

"No," I said as I hugged my knees to my chest. I missed him with every ounce of my soul. He had been the first part of my day, the last part of my day, and every thought in between for months. And then it was all ripped out from under me.

"Jurnee?" Marina said softly. "Which one are you saying no to?"

"I want to patch things up, but I don't know how it's possible. He won't tell his family about me, isn't that a big deal?"

"But you *love* him, Jurnee. Try talking to him and seeing if he still feels the same way. Or do you want one of us to talk to him for you?"

I shook my head silently.

"If you love him, you have to at least try." Marina did have a point. I felt so defeated, though.

"I know. But it's more than just this," I started.

Krista jumped in without a second, "What else happened?"

"I'm the wrong nationality. I'm the wrong religion. I don't know his family's language. He's right. I can't fit in."

"He said that?" Krista was taken aback.

"Not exactly. But maybe we're too different." I was still devastated, but in that moment, I truly resigned hope of ever getting back together.

The days started melting together. Some days, I wouldn't eat. Some nights, I wouldn't sleep. But one thing remained – Anooj was always in the back of my mind. Sometimes, I thought about calling him or texting him, but I couldn't bring myself to.

That night, I got a friend request on Facebook. There was just a first name and photo was of a celebrity, so I disregarded it. About an hour later, I got a message into my "other" folder.

Hello, is this Jurnee Ryan? the message read.

Who is this? I asked, thoroughly confused.

Myself Devi, she messaged with an assortment of emojis. *Tell me something about you.*

It was Anooj's sister.

My stomach dropped, and I had no idea what to say. How had they found out about me? *Hi, sure,* I started. *Anything specific?*

Send more photos. I wasn't sure what to send, so I sent a variety. Photos from Kerala, with my family, as a child. Maybe this was the first step to getting Anooj back; I had to treat this as an interview.

Do you know Tamil? she asked. *Why were you in Kerala? Do you know Malayalam?*

I was teaching English in a village called Kumbalam.

Now something about your character. And your eating habits and good habits.

This was definitely an interview. The fact that I'm vegetarian had gone over really well with everyone in Kerala, so I was sure to mention it. I wasn't sure what was meant by good habits, though.

That is fine. Anooj will eat anything that is not an aeroplane or ship. Now tell about your family.

I have my two parents and some extended family, I mentioned.

Where?

In my house with me.

Good. Do you know cooking? Your favorite foods?

I was so nervous about messing up. This was probably my only real chance to get Anooj back. I had to convince her that my nationality and religion and language didn't matter. *I can follow recipes and quite enjoy most anything with potato or cauliflower.*

What is your job? What are your parents' jobs?

I am a teacher. My mother works in insurance, and my father is an engineer.

How much do you like my brother?

Moment of truth. *I like him a lot,* I said honestly. These past few weeks had been absolutely dreadful, and I missed him terribly.

What do you know about him?

He is a very good person. Kind, patient, smart.

When is your next trip to India? Does my brother like you?

I was planning to come in December but no plan now. Did he like me anymore? I honestly wasn't sure. *I don't think he likes me anymore.*

He does very much. For past two weeks he is only talking about you to everyone.

Wait. He had finally told his family? This was huge. If I did this right, everything would be fine and we could get back together. *Calm down, Jurnee,* I told myself. *Don't get too excited. This doesn't mean anything yet. Don't count your chickens before they hatch.*

With a deep breath, I continued. *Oh.*

So, when can be the marriage?

Just like that? Did I pass? Was that it? Anooj had been right about the sudden planning. *Anytime is ok.* I didn't want to push my luck and be picky. I just hoped that this really meant what I thought it meant. Tears fell, but for the happiest possible reason. Should I call Anooj?

We will discuss and let you know.

Now it was the waiting game. I read back through the messages to make sure that I had done okay with the interview. I think I passed. I just had to wait and see.

The next few days went by painstakingly slowly. I was back in the habit of starting and stopping a thousand messages to Anooj. Whenever I saw him online, I could feel myself subconsciously stop breathing. Would he say something?

Finally, I gave up on him. *Hello?* I messaged him.

I instantly scolded myself. Why did I do that? *Jurnee, my voice of reason kicked in. Someone has to make the first move. You can't just wait forever. What if you regret not saying anything later?* I did have a point. For a brief moment, I wondered if other people's thoughts argued with themselves to the point of having full conversations, but I shrugged it off.

I told them, he said. *I told everyone.*

What happened?

I couldn't not be with you, Jurnee. I was miserable without you.

Me too, I said.

I mean really *miserable. I couldn't eat, couldn't sleep.*

Neither could I.

So, I told my family. You know how it is.

I didn't, but I said I did. There were enough differences being highlighted right now, I didn't want to add any more to the list.

You talking to my sister really helped. My mom is almost convinced.

So, what do we do now?

We wait.

Waiting was nerve-wracking. At least when I thought it was over, there was a conclusion that I could tell myself, even if it was horrible. But now it was uncertain. We were so close, but we had no idea if we would make it through.

What if they say no?

He started and stopped typing a few times. This was bad. *Let's try to think positively.*

It was admirable that he felt so strongly that we shouldn't marry against anyone's wishes, but what about me? Or maybe I was being selfish, and his respectful Indian mentality was more correct. *When will we know?* I asked.

Soon. My sister really likes you, though, so I think she can convince my mother. Don't worry.

I was mildly relieved but still very much worried. And his calm front did nothing to calm me, it actually made me much more worried. Why was he so calm? Did he not care either way?

Can I call you? he asked.

Since when do you need to ask? He had never asked before, why now?

Not even a second later, my phone began to chirp. It was just like old times, like the last two weeks had been completely erased. Everything was perfect. We laughed all night. He always knew how to make me laugh, even when I was upset or anxious. Somehow more than my parents, even more than Krista and Marina.

I woke up to my phone ringing. "Oh no," I thought. "Was that all a dream?" My heart fell into the pit of my stomach as I realized that the entire thing had been a dream. Anooj, Devi, our long call after weeks of silence. None of it had happened.

Looking closely at the screen, I realized that it was Anooj calling. Had I manifested this, or had it not been a dream after all?

"Hello?" I said with the froggiest morning voice that I couldn't disguise.

"Jurnee? Are you awake?"

"I am now," I said, a bit annoyed. I opened my messages to see if it had really happened. The conversation with Anooj was there, the conversation with Devi was there. It wasn't a dream.

"Jurnee, I have to tell you something."

No. No. No. No. No. I just knew that they had said no, and everything was cancelled.

"Jurnee, are you sitting down?"

"Well, laying. But yeah, why?"

"Jurnee we're getting married."

Was he proposing? "Sorry, what?"

"My sister convinced my mom, so they went to speak to the priest, and he said the auspicious time is the 15th of May. We're getting married."

"May 15th of *next year*?" I asked for clarity. That was in six months.

"Yes."

Holy. Shit. We were getting married. Officially.

CHAPTER 4

But we're not even engaged! How can we have a wedding date?" He had been right all along, this *was* moving extremely fast. "My parents don't know we're that serious yet. I haven't even spoken to your mom."

"You will, but you need to learn a bit of Tamil first. She is shy to speak English."

I made a note to search for a Tamil tutor right away. That had been one of the factors against us, and she had agreed despite it. I was going to learn Tamil for her.

I had said I was ready, but now that the time came I wasn't completely sure that I was. Backing down could compromise things later and it wasn't an option. If I didn't proceed carefully, everything would be ruined. I knew that I loved him and that I'd never felt this way for anyone before. I trusted him and could completely be myself around him. He was calm, patient, and caring. He would make an excellent husband and an excellent father, in time.

But this was all happening now, and if I waited, it would all be ruined. It was now or never, and I had to do whatever it took.

We talked for a bit more before I resigned myself to looking for ways to learn Tamil. I glanced through some book PDFs that I saw online, but it looked so complicated. They had completely different letters, and some of the sounds weren't even in English. They had drawings of tongue placements for different letters, and it all seemed way beyond my skill level. I would have to learn to decode the alphabet of another language and somehow speak it as well; this was going to be much more difficult than high school Spanish.

I began to search for an app. There were only a handful, and I tried all of them, but none really helped. I decided to look into tutors. Guided classes in a one-on-one setting would definitely allow me to learn more quickly and effectively, plus it would help my pronunciation to be able to have direct guidance.

The resources for learning Tamil were abysmal. Hundreds available for Spanish, Chinese, Arabic, yet hardly any for Tamil. I stumbled upon a tutoring site and went through the list of Tamil tutors. They each had an introduction video, and they all seemed very good. One in particular caught my eye. He spoke very calmly, but confidently, and I thought he would be perfect. It was a little more than I wanted to spend, but this was important. I immediately booked a demo class.

Good morning, Jurnee, read a WhatsApp message that came in from Devi. *How was your day?*

It was good. How was your sleep?

Not able to get sleep.

Oh no, any problem?

All okay, just not getting sleep. Tell me.

Tell you what? Every time I felt more confident in this new dialect, I found more things that I didn't know. How could I learn a new dialect *and* a new language? *You can do it, Jurnee,* I said in a silent pep talk to myself. *Rome wasn't built in a day.* I was right, I just needed to take it slow.

Anything.

I just registered for Tamil class.

Ohhh, super! Glad to hear.

She tried to teach me a few basic words, but it was difficult to grasp without proper instruction. Another thought burst into my mind, "This is the perfect opportunity to buy a new notebook." Ever since childhood, I loved back to school season, not for going back to school, but for buying heaps of new school supplies. There was nothing like the first pen stroke on the first page of a fresh notebook.

We continued chatting for a while until she stopped replying, so I assumed that she had slept. Tonight would be my first Tamil class. I was afraid of how difficult it may be, but happy to be taking the first steps to fit in better with his family.

That night when I logged into the tutoring website, I was met by my new teacher, Priyan.

"Good evening, Jurnee, how was your day?"

"Good, what about yours?"

"Good, good. So, why is it that you're wanting to learn Tamil?" he asked.

I had to whisper since my parents didn't totally know yet, "Actually I'm getting married next year, and his family speaks Tamil."

"Fantastic!" he said enthusiastically. "Are you wanting to know just how to speak, or are you interested in reading and writing as well?"

"I feel like my primary emphasis should be on speaking, but since the alphabet is phonetic, I would like to learn to read and write just to make sure I have the correct pronunciation."

"Nice idea, we will do just that. Have you learned any Tamil words at all yet?"

"Just a few basics, but nothing substantial."

"Alright then, let's get started with a couple of basic L sounds."

I opened my notebook and clicked my pen; I was officially learning Tamil.

"There are three L sounds. The first is your basic English *la* where you place your tongue at the corner where your top teeth meet the roof of your mouth," he said as he demonstrated it a couple of times and had me follow suit. "Next is slightly different. I will often denote this with a capital L when I am writing words for you. It is pronounced my placing your tongue in the middle-back area of the roof of your mouth," he said with another demonstration as I also practiced. "Lastly is the *zha,* in which you will place your tongue back in your throat and simply make a sound."

"But isn't that more of an R sound?"

"For us, this is L only."

I shrugged it off and took my first notes – the three Ls.

"Let's try one after the other – *la, La, zha*."

"Ok – *la, La, zha*."

"Perfect!"

Really? Maybe Tamil wouldn't be so hard.

"Now let's learn some basic pronouns."

Class continued and, surprisingly, I didn't find it overly difficult. I hoped that I would do well and be able to continue to eventual fluency. I just had to be patient and study hard. This wasn't Spanish class in high school that I only took to get the credits. This was real life, and I had very practical use for it. My future was pretty dependent on having a good grasp of it.

After class, I made my way downstairs for family dinner. It was usually one of the most relaxing times of day, but now that I was apparently getting married in just a few months, suddenly I was extremely nervous. How would I tell them? If we'd gone the typical American Christian way, I'd have a ring to show to make an announcement, but something about this just felt so odd and out of order. I decided not to say anything until we were officially engaged, in case his family changed their minds.

As soon as I sat down, I noticed how oddly they were behaving. My dad was staring at me the way you stare at the ball right before they cover it with a cup and start mixing them around – a mixture of mostly excitement, but a little bit of fear. My mother looked very emotional. "Is everything ok?" I asked them.

"Everything is perfect," my mother replied.

"Did you see another movie on the Hallmark Channel?" I asked her. She had a thing for sappy unrealistic romcoms.

"No," she said defensively. She hated when I teased her about those movies. "You're just growing up so fast."

"That's what we mammals do," I replied. This felt so awkward. "I think I'm going to go and eat upstairs."

"No, you will not, young lady," my father said sternly.

"…Okay?" I said with a brief pause. What was going on?

"So, tell us about your day. Is anything new? How is Anooj? What are Krista and Marina up to these days?"

Did they know? "Nothing new, all of us are fine."

They looked back at me suspiciously. Something was definitely happening.

"Okay then," my mom tried again. "How is school?"

"It's good. My students are all really great."

"Do you ever miss your students in India?"

"All the time," I said with a tinge of sadness. I still thought about them every day. They were such amazing kids, and I loved them dearly. Some of them still chatted with me on WhatsApp or Facebook occasionally.

"Do you plan to go back and see them? And to see Anooj?"

"Probably over Christmas break since I'll have so much time off. I hope you guys don't mind me missing Christmas this year."

"We completely understand. You should go and have fun," my dad confirmed.

I was lucky to have such supportive parents. We continued dinner with a lighter chat, discussing what the plans were for Thanksgiving in a couple of weeks and about the new couch my mom was thinking about buying.

When I looked at them, I saw Anooj and I. Is that how we would be in thirty years? Figuring out what to do for the holidays and debating couch colors? It was so comfortable and relaxed.

Dinner ended, and I had planned to stay downstairs to watch TV with my parents, but Anooj had woken up. My parents could tell by my sudden interest in my phone and bid me goodnight as I went upstairs.

"Good morning, Jurnee Miss," he said like a school kid, with a lilt to his voice. "How was the day?"

"Fine, but my parents are acting super weird."

"What do you mean?"

"My mom is like weird and emotional, and my dad keeps staring at me."

"Just today? Suddenly?"

"Yeah, it's so weird."

He started laughing super awkwardly. "Actually, it's not *that* weird."

"What do you mean?" I asked accusingly.

"Well, I kind of called them before I went to sleep. With my mom."

"I haven't met your mother, but my parents have?"

"That's how it is here. Our parents have to first meet. I was just there to translate."

"So, what happened? What did you talk about?" I was so curious and had a thousand questions. I needed to be caught up immediately.

"So, first I called them to ask their blessing for us to get engaged. I saw online that it is an American custom. Then my mother had to meet them to make sure that they were good people and to make sure that they were okay with our union also."

It sounded so formal, more like a business transaction than a wedding.

"So, now we have just about six months to plan everything. My mom and sister will handle most everything; you'll just need to give your preference for foods and dresses, get your ticket, and figure out who is coming so that we can prepare for their arrival."

"Probably just my parents and Krista and Marina. I'm not super close to anyone else to justify them spending a thousand dollars to come across the world for a wedding."

"Okay, no problem. I'll let my family know. Are you still coming over Christmas? I thought we could get formally engaged then."

No one was in front of me, but I could still feel my face redden as I looked down. It was happening so much more easily than I had anticipated.

"Are you nervous about meeting my family at all?"

"No," I lied.

"Jurnee, you can't fool me," he teased. "I know you will be. Don't be worried, though, they will love you just as I do."

It was sweet but did nothing for my absolute terror at the thought of meeting his family. One bad first impression and I could forever ruin my relationship with the people who would be my second family. They seemed nice from what I knew of them. I was just afraid of making a mistake and accidentally offending them or making them regret their approval.

"Just be yourself. A more formal version of yourself, but overall, yourself."

"Should I bring anything, like gifts or something?"

"No, they are not so much into gifts. Don't worry about it."

"But isn't it rude to come empty-handed? I should at least bring like chocolates or something."

"It's really not needed. Relax."

"Fine," I said with a sigh. This was going to be the biggest interview of my life. I'd seen in movies how perfectly acceptable people were rejected by Indian families for silly reasons. What if they changed their minds after meeting me? That was one of the main reasons why I was so hesitant to tell my family until after things were completely sorted. I was terrified; everything was out of my hands.

One lesson I'd learned from Malayalam and Tamil movies was that romantic movies didn't end when the lead actors fell in love, there was always the task of convincing their families as well. My life was slowly becoming an Indian film.

"Soon you will be Jurnee Anooj," he said happily.

"Wait, what?"

"Jurnee Anooj."

But that was his first name. "Don't you mean Jurnee Dhakshinamurthy?"

"No, that is my father's name. You will be Jurnee Anooj only. We don't have family names; surname comes from the father or husband."

Jurnee Dhakshinamurthy sounded a lot smoother than Jurnee Anooj, but if I took his last name, I guess that would kind of make me his sister instead of his wife. "Oh," I said, not knowing what else to say. I wasn't against the idea; it was just a very new concept.

I remembered back to my school in Kerala and how the students all asked if my father's name was Ryan since that was my last name. I had thought it was odd then, but it all made sense now. I was to be *Jurnee Anooj*.

The next day at school, Devi texted me. *Jurnee, think and tell what kind of invitations you want.*

My first task as an unofficial bride-to-be, how exciting.

Browsing through Google, I saw a lot of simple and cute invitations. Golden calligraphy swirls contrasting a deep burgundy finish, custom cartoons of couples in wedding attire, plain invitations, big invitations with lots of details and passages, some even had the couples' degree information on it. *For what?* I thought to myself. Was that necessary? A bit invasive, to say the least.

We settled on two different kinds. A simple pink one with white leaves for close friends, and a massive golden booklet with a lot of traditional symbolism on it for family and formal invites. It seemed odd to me that they had to be different, but perhaps that was normal. I was learning a lot about letting go of my expectations. Growing up entirely in American culture, I was seeing that many things I thought were normal were unheard of elsewhere. A white wedding dress, for one, was entirely out of the question.

That evening, I booked my tickets for India. I had almost two weeks off for Christmas, and it was going to be hectic. Meeting Anooj's family, getting engaged, going back to my village in Kerala to see everyone again, and doing some sightseeing. After all, it was still a vacation. I was most excited to see Anooj again, though. After everything we'd been through, I couldn't wait to see him again. And this time, we would be together for the entire time, not just a few days or hours here and there.

It had been a bit more than I'd wanted to pay, but I was booking very late in the game. I should have booked weeks ago, and now I was paying much more than I did for the ticket to Kerala. Or was it because flying into Madurai was more expensive since it was a smaller airport than Trivandrum? Or was it because tickets during the holidays always cost more due to peak season pricing? I guess it was a bit of everything, but it was still much more than I had anticipated paying. At least I was still living at home, so it wasn't completely awful.

At dinner I made the announcement to my parents. "My tickets are December 23 to January 4."

My mother had that weird emotional look in her eyes again. I knew that she knew what was going to happen. "It's no problem at all, sweetie," she said as she took my hand in hers.

"We'll just celebrate late, it's okay," my dad said with a hint of a mischievous smile. We were both trying to hide from the other that we knew exactly what was going to happen. It was almost comical.

In the coming weeks, I made preparations for my trip back to India. I bought lots of gourmet chocolates to distribute amongst my students. I bought some for Anooj's family as well, despite receiving warnings against it. I didn't want to come empty-handed, even if he said it was okay. I had to ace this interview because there were no backup choices. This was a thousand times more high stakes than any other interview I'd had.

I wasn't excited to go to India like last time. I felt physically ill. I'd never been so nervous about anything in my entire life.

When my parents dropped me off at the airport, they knew something was wrong. "Is everything okay, dear?" my mother asked.

"Just nervous about flying again," I said with a chuckle, trying to throw her off the scent. She had that creepy all-knowing smile again, there was no disguising what was really happening.

We all got out of the car as my dad went around back to get my suitcase out. "Well, tell everyone hello from us," he said as he sat it on the ground, ready for me to wheel it away.

"Will do," I said with a smile as I tried to conceal my shivering. I had decided against packing a coat since I knew I wouldn't need it for more than a few minutes.

They reached out to hug me as I looked around again at the brown tree skeletons coated in snow. It was exactly like it had been last year, and I knew that when I stepped out of the airport, I would be transported to a warm place with sprawling greenery. Well, at least it had been that way in Kerala. If Tamil Nadu was the neighboring state, it must be somewhat similar.

They broke away from the hug and slowly made their way back to their seats. "Bye, Jurnee. We love you. Be safe," my dad called from the passenger seat.

"Call us when you get there! Last time, you were extremely irresponsible in your texting!" I guess she was right. I had tried to explain that there was almost no signal, but she wouldn't accept that as an excuse. Maybe there would be better signal in a city.

"Love you guys, bye!" I called as I made my way to the entrance of O'Hare's Terminal 5. With a deep breath, I passed through the sliding glass door. Next time I was in America, I would be engaged.

CHAPTER 5

Stepping out of the airport, I was struck by how everything seemed the same yet different. I was only about three hundred miles away from Kumbalam, but it was almost as if I were in a different country.

Looking into the distance, there didn't seem to be as much greenery. Everything else looked the same: black and yellow *autos*, women in *sarees*, men in *mundus...* though Anooj had told me that they were called *veshtis* here. They seemed to follow the same unspoken rule as in Kerala, wherein the younger generation largely wore jeans instead. But unlike Trivandrum, it seemed women of all ages wore *sarees*, even young professional looking women. And they all had the jasmine flowers in their hair that I had worn for Annual Day. *Is it a special occasion?* I wondered to myself.

The letters also looked slightly different. When in Kerala, Malayalam letters on every signboard had rounded edges and most had swirls. Tamil letters, I noticed, were much more boxy. They shared many similarities, there was a letter that looked like headphones turned to the side in each language, but overall, there were many stark differences. It was incredible to me how two cities in relatively close proximity could have so many differences, even a different *language*. That was unbelievable.

The air was just as heavy and humid, the smell of my cousin's incense still hung in the air. It was like I was in a parallel universe, and I half-wondered if I was in the wrong place until I saw Anooj.

Standing at the edge of the gate, he looked to me, beaming. It had been nine months since I last saw him, but he looked so different. I'd seen his new beard in video calls, but it hadn't really clicked that he really had one. It looked great on him, just a bit of long stubble.

I couldn't believe that this was finally happening. Everything was perfect now, and soon, we would be engaged. It felt odd that I already knew it was happening, but I chalked it up to cultural differences and tried to not dwell too much on the mild disappointment of knowing that I would never have a surprise engagement. At least we would be together; nothing else mattered.

I ran into his arms, and we stood in a firm, prolonged hug, despite the glaring disapproval from those around us. "I missed you," he whispered down to me.

I was already dreading being away from him for five months after this trip was over. *Live in the moment, Jurnee,* I scolded myself. *Enjoy yourself now, stop thinking about later.*

He took my suitcase as we started walking to his car. I wanted to look around and take in this incredible new place. I had now been to two Indian states! But I couldn't stop staring at him. I was really here. We were really together.

"So, what do you want to do first?" he asked but it instantly took me back to right before I left Trivandrum. When my flight was delayed, and we were trying to figure out how to spend the next three hours. It was like Déjà vu.

Once reminded of those last three hours, all I could think about was *dosa* and *Mysore Pak*. "*Dosa*?" I suggested coyly.

"Do you want to take rest or freshen up or anything?"

I didn't want to be away from him for a single moment. "No, I'm fine. Let's go," I said as he lifted my suitcase into the back of the car.

He walked around the car and jokingly opened my door with a bow, "Ok, Jurnee Madam, let us go."

I couldn't help but to laugh, "You're such a dork," I teased him.

Driving through Tamil Nadu, I continued to be taken in by the bizarre mixture of things that were exactly the same yet also so different. I heard people calling out words like *po* and *vaa* which I had come to learn in Kerala as meaning *go* and *come*, but they also used them here.

"Is today a holiday?" I asked him.

"No, just a regular day. Why, what happened?"

"Nothing happened. Just seeing everyone with jasmine in their hair like we had for Annual Day."

"That is Madurai style," he said with a chuckle. "Every Madurai *ponnu* will have. Do you want some?"

"Maybe tomorrow. I look like an absolute mess right now."

"No, Jurnee. You are beautiful."

When I turned to smile at him, I realized how lucky I was. Somehow, against all odds, I had found this absolutely incredible person in a different hemisphere. We never would have met if I hadn't taken that random chance to teach at a school in an Indian village. I had never believed in fate, but there was no other explanation for it.

The *dosa* was just as I remembered it. Simultaneously oily and crispy. This time I wasn't shy about smothering it in tomato chutney. I had tried no less than ten Indian restaurants back home, but none compared to this one. It was a little bit spicier than it had been in Kerala, but it was absolutely heavenly. My tolerance for spicy food had increased drastically since living in the hostel, and I wasn't even thirsty while eating it.

The stares continued to permeate my skull, but I tried my best to ignore them. I kept reminding myself that they weren't staring at *me*, they were just curious.

"I'll just wash my hands and come," he said as he stood to go to the hand wash station. Looking down at my right hand, I realized that I should probably wash, too, since I'd actually eaten *dosa* the proper way this time. Thinking back to my first time when I'd tried dunking it like chips and salsa, I couldn't help but to laugh. No wonder that waiter had come to help. I must have looked so silly.

One thing I quite liked about restaurants in India was that there was a place to wash your hands that was not directly connected to a bathroom. The bad thing about restaurants in India was that the bathrooms I'd encountered were often unlit and didn't generally have toilet paper.

"Ready?" he asked as we approached the table.

"Where to next?" I asked, secretly hoping that he knew a place around here as good as Sri Krishna Sweets had been.

"*Mysore Pak*?" he asked hopefully. He knew me far too well.

I didn't even have to say anything. My face instantly lit up at the very mention, and I jumped in the car, ready to be reunited with my beloved *Mysore Pak*.

We drove to a thin, crowded street and parked a few shops away.

If it weren't for the boxy Tamil letters and more people wearing traditional clothing, I wouldn't notice that I wasn't in Kerala. I wondered what other differences I would find sprinkled along the way.

"So, why did you guys move back?"

"To be closer to family. We don't really have a lot of connections in Trivandrum, and my sister's family is here. Remember, she has a daughter too, so we just wanted to be closer."

"Which do you like better?"

"Trivandrum is fun. I made a lot of new friends, had a decent job, it was beautiful. But nothing beats home. My childhood friends are here, I work in an MNC that has an office here too, so I just had to transfer. Here we have *jigarthanda* and Meenakshi Temple. I like Trivandrum a lot, definitely I'll visit sometimes, but Madurai is my soul."

"What is *jiggertinda*?" I asked with a horrendous mispronunciation, vaguely remembering it being mentioned earlier.

"It's the best ice cream you'll ever eat in your life."

My interest was piqued. I smiled as we walked into Sri Krishna Sweets. How was India only famous for spicy food when the desserts were so delicious?

At first I was shocked that it was here too, but the sign on the wall showed that it was in several cities. There was a place called Coimbatore that had more than a dozen of them. I was instantly jealous of everyone who lived there.

The counters looked exactly the same, the decadent sweets taking up every square inch in the display. The employees stood patiently waiting for us to walk up and make our request. Without hesitation, as though he was a childhood friend, I called to the man at the counter, "Two samples of *Mysore Pak*, please."

Anooj laughed at me, and the attendant did his best to conceal his laughter as well. I couldn't wait any longer. It had been months since I'd had it, and nothing could stand in my way. He cut off small slivers and sat them on the counter.

It melted in my mouth, just as I had remembered. I would happily gain five hundred pounds to have some every day of my life.

"Any other sample, madam?" the attendant asked. He smiled to Anooj as well, amused that a foreigner was so enthusiastic about their sweets.

"I'll have *Chikki, Soan Papdi*, and," I hesitated. "Anooj what was the other one? The long name brown one?"

"*Tirunelveli Halwa*," he said to the attendant.

"You have good taste in Indian sweets, madam," he said over the counter.

"Thank you," I said back. I was mildly embarrassed by how hyper I was being, but I was so excited. It had been so long since I'd had these sweets, and I needed to eat all of them immediately.

"Don't forget to save room for *jigarthanda,*" Anooj reminded me.

"Giving her the full tour, *aa*? Which tour company are you with?" the attendant asked Anooj.

Anooj smiled, "Actually, we are getting married."

The whole shop turned to look at us. "Wow! Many congratulations to both of you."

We thanked the attendant in unison before Anooj turned to the man again, "We'll have one *kg* parcel of *Mysore Pak.*" It always struck me how people here spoke abbreviations instead of the full form, like *k.g.* for kilogram or *g.b.* for gigabyte.

"Why so much?" I whispered to him.

"My family will want some also," he said. I instantly felt stupid. Of course they did, it was delicious.

We went back to the car, and before I knew it, we had parked at a small shop Anooj claimed to be world famous. It didn't look world famous.

While walking over to the small shop, I noticed a billboard for a car. It said that it was ₹3,26,000. "Anooj?"

"Yes, Jurnee Madam," he said with a laugh as I rolled my eyes.

"Why did they put an extra comma in the ad? Shouldn't it say ₹326,000?"

"No. This is *lakhs*, not dollars. We will write like this only."

I was still confused, but I knew that differences here were better managed by going with the tide than against the tide. It had been this way for centuries, and I was just one little blob on her second trip here. The times

I'd struggled most with adapting to this new culture were times that I didn't take the time to appreciate the differences. In those difficult moments, I had been the one to make them difficult by assuming that I was right and pushing my own ideals on everything else. Like the rice saga in the hostel. I needed to accept the *lakh* the way I accepted eating rice three times a day.

Anooj had ordered for us while I was having another monologue in my head. Soon we were both served what looked to be an ice cream float in tall cylindrical glasses. They weren't the usual stainless steel that everyone used, they were proper glass. Rather than a straw inside, there was a spoon.

It was brown, so I assumed that it would be chocolate, but it wasn't. I hadn't quite had anything that tasted similar to it before and searched fruitlessly for a way to describe it. It was good, but I couldn't place the taste.

"How do they make this?" I asked Anooj as we stood to the side of the small shop.

He started listing out ingredients I'd never heard of, so there was no chance of me placing the taste.

"How is it?" he asked.

"Great!" Not being able to place the taste was driving me crazy though.

"This is very famous here, you know. No one can come to Madurai without having *jigarthanda*," he said as we got back into the car. "Are you okay?" he asked, noticing my silence.

I wasn't. I was absolutely terrified of the high stakes meeting with his family. If I did poorly, everything would be ruined. Luckily, I had brought some Ghirardelli chocolate squares and prayed silently that they would like them, and me.

My anxiety was getting the best of me and, no less than three times, I had to ask Anooj to pull over because I thought that I would vomit.

"Don't take so much tension, Jurnee. They love me so they will love you, too. And you've been chatting with my sister so much, don't worry like this."

I couldn't help it, though. This was bigger than the ACT, bigger than college acceptances, bigger than my interviews. This was what would truly determine my entire future. I had never been under so much pressure. These weren't American parents who I could easily charm with a smile and cupcakes. This was a completely different culture with customs and unspoken rules that I had never learned.

Back home, I had tried to Google some helpful articles about winning over Indian parents, but many of them only told unsuccessful stories and worst-case scenarios. What was meant to give me more tips and ideas only served to further discourage me.

One article had helped immensely. Well, I couldn't be certain of it yet, but I was hopeful. It said that the primary thing Indian parents were worried about when their child marries outside of the culture is that they will lose their roots and, subsequently, so will their grandchildren. My interpretation of this was that if I didn't learn Tamil, our children wouldn't be able to speak Tamil well, and thus they would have difficulty interacting with Anooj's family. So, by taking on this small task of learning his language, I was ensuring future generations would not lose their connection to their roots.

Luckily, my Tamil studies were going pretty well, and I was slowly making my way to being able to build basic sentences. Understanding what people were saying was still tough, but I was steadily improving.

It also specifically said never to show any affection with each other in front of parents. Not even an arm pat or hand hold; we were to always maintain distance. It said to bring gifts, but Anooj said not to. I guess it was better to follow his advice rather than the advice of the internet, but I figured that chocolates were at least a happy medium.

We arrived at Devi's house after several twists and turns through a narrow bumpy road. There was an ornate black gate in the front and a small sitting area between the gate and the front door. A swing hung beside a set of stairs that appeared to lead to a terrace. A colorful design beside the swing was made of powder, and several shoes also sat just outside the door of the two-story cement house. It reminded me of the houses in Kerala, except that it was just plain white and not a bright color.

Please don't hate me. Please don't hate me. Please don't hate me, I silently begged.

Anooj rang the doorbell that, surprisingly, was not a bell at all. It sounded like an army of birds chirping. An army of birds attacking the butterflies in my stomach and making me feel sick.

Chapter 6

A young girl answered the door and shouted for her parents. She was his nine-year-old niece, Aarthi. She stared at me intensely, but I wasn't sure if it was positively or negatively until she grabbed my hand enthusiastically to play with her. She pulled me past their living room and into her bedroom to reveal numerous toys scattered across the floor. There were dolls of various sizes, a supermarket, and a Play-Doh hair salon.

"I am Aarthi," she announced.

"Hi Aarthi. I'm Jurnee," I said, hoping that this would be as easy as it had been at school.

"I know," she said smugly. Of course she knew. Out of the corner of my eye, I saw Anooj taking my suitcase in a small room connected to the living room.

Soon we were joined by her parents and Anooj, who came to join us on the floor. They all seemed to be studying me. This was my test of how well I interacted with Aarthi. I was nervous but tried to maintain my composure through this evaluation in hopes that I made it to the next round, meeting Anooj's mom. The whole time I had that nervous feeling, like when you think you may poop at any time.

"So, Jurnee," Devi began with a slight smirk. "How was the journey?"

"Good," I smiled. "It wasn't too long, and we just got back from having *dosa*, *Mysore Pak*, and *jigarthanda*."

She looked at Anooj, aghast. "Then what will we eat for dinner? You knew that we were preparing for her arrival," she stared at him angrily until her husband said something softly to her in Tamil. He seemed very jovial, and she seemed to be as nervous as I was. Luckily, it helped me to relax just a bit knowing that I wasn't the only one.

Her husband, Naren, and Aarthi went to the kitchen to get the food and plates and brought them back to the bedroom floor where we were playing. They were the metal cake pan plates just like in the hostel. There were short metal tumblers for water also. All the memories came flooding back to me, and I yearned to see my students. It would be just another week or so until I could, since they were also having their Christmas break.

"*Aththai*," Aarthi started as she scooped the food onto her plate. "Why do you like *mama*?"

"*Mama*?" I silently mouthed to Anooj, confused.

"Uncle," he whispered. That didn't ease my confusion at all, though.

She was still looking at me for an answer. Should I tell her about how nice he was, or how patient he was, or how calm he was, or how cute he looked in a *veshti*? "I like his *gunam*," I told her, opting to use one of my Tamil vocabulary words, which meant *character*.

"Oooh," she said with surprise. "*Thamizh theriyumaa?*"

"*Konjam,*" I replied, indicating that I knew only a small bit of Tamil.

She smiled and continued eating.

"What is this?" I asked as I scooped some dark orange soup beside my *parottas*.

"*Salna,*" Devi replied. "Tamil special."

It tasted a bit like a spicier, thinner tomato soup. It was delicious, but I had no appetite. Somehow Anooj was still eating enthusiastically, and I had no idea how.

I could feel myself being observed, so I tried to eat as carefully as I could with my hands.

"*Aththai,* do this like," Aarthi said as she held out her hand to give a demonstration. There was a critical error in my technique. Without realizing it, I was always keeping my index finger pointing outwards rather than using it to pinch the soaked *parotta* with all five fingers.

"How is our Tamil food?" Devi asked.

"Amazing," I replied enthusiastically.

I had come so far, yet I still had so far to go.

"And what do you think of our Madurai?" she asked.

"It's beautiful. I can't wait to see more of it."

"Anooj, you must take her for shopping tomorrow."

A surge of excitement. Shopping in India was very stressful, but immeasurably fun. You never knew what treasures awaited you. "What are we shopping for?" I asked them.

"Dresses for you," Aarthi said cheerily.

I secretly hoped that I would be able to wear a saree again but didn't want to inconvenience anyone, since I would need help to wear it. More than this would be the awkwardness of being half naked in front of people I hoped would be my future in-laws, but who I hadn't actually known for very long.

One by one, we finished eating. I followed Anooj with plate and cup and imitated him as he washed his hands. "I'll see you tomorrow," he said as we walked back to the room.

"What do you mean? You're leaving?" That was why he had brought my suitcase.

"I have to go home. I'll be back in the morning to take you for shopping."

Sullenly, I watched him bid goodnight to Aarthi and her parents as he walked outside and drove away. We continued sitting on the floor of Aarthi's bedroom when her father pulled out a projector from behind the door. Judging by her excitement, he had put on her favorite – a Tamil dubbed version of *Home Alone*.

"Did you bring us any sweets from America?" she asked as I immediately jumped up and went to fetch them from my suitcase. I'd almost forgotten.

Coming back to the room, Aarthi beamed as Devi got up to bring pillows and blankets to all of us, and we lay in the dark watching and eating chocolates together. *I hope I'm doing well,* I thought to myself, but it wasn't long until I'd drifted off to sleep. Being nervous was exhausting.

The next morning, I woke up much earlier than everyone else, perhaps due to jetlag. I scolded myself for sleeping without removing my contacts or washing my face but decided to check my phone instead. A WhatsApp message to Anooj, a quick text to update my parents, some scrolling through Facebook, but then I realized…

I was in India again, and Anooj wouldn't be awake. We were in the same time zone now.

That was one convenient thing about being in a long-distance relationship – anytime I couldn't sleep, I knew that he would be awake to chat with me until I dozed off again. There wasn't any chance of that now.

It was only 4 a.m., and I was bored out of my mind. I downloaded a cooking game on my phone with the tight deadlines and angry customers, the perfect way to pass time.

After three hours and dozens of levels, they began to wake up. I was half excited to not be alone anymore, but half nervous since the interview would resume. Anooj hadn't texted me back yet, so I was on my own.

"Get fresh and come," Aarthi said with the excitement that only a child possesses immediately after waking up.

"Where is the bathroom?" I asked Devi.

"Just there," she pointed with a nod of her head towards the living room. I decided to go into the room where Anooj had left my suitcase and see if maybe that was where the bathroom was.

Walking inside the room, it was an unused second bedroom with a few dolls and books, but it seemed to be a guest room. I immediately felt guilty. Should I have slept here last night instead? Was I invading their space by sharing their room? Had they not meant for me to fall asleep there, and I was being rude?

Shut up, Jurnee, I scolded myself as I opened my suitcase to get out my toiletries. Rummaging through my jeans, shirts, chocolates, and other various items, I finally found my toiletry bag.

I pushed open what I assumed to be the bathroom door and walked into a most peculiar room. There was a standard American toilet, a standard Indian toilet, a shower with water heater, and another small spout beside the Indian toilet. It made sense, wanting to accommodate any guest's preferences by offering inclusive options, but it was still somewhat shocking at first glance.

I had wanted to take a shower the minute I landed since I had that grimy airplane feeling, but it hadn't been possible. I'd wanted to at least have a shower before sleeping, but I wasn't comfortable enough yet to ask about it. I felt cleaner with every drop of water, and I relished in it.

Anooj must have told them my favorites because waiting for me in the living room was fresh *vada* with tomato and coconut chutney. I was starving, and they looked delicious.

They were just as I had remembered. Crispy on the outside, soft and spicy on the inside.

"How is it?" Naren asked.

The answer was evident by my eyes being closed in absolute ecstasy, but I answered nonetheless. "Good," I replied, too nervous to practice my Tamil.

He nodded his head in acknowledgement and continued eating his, but I was full after just three. Enviously watching them each finish off four and five *vada* each made me wish I had an endless appetite.

"Have more," Devi gestured towards the remaining two *vada* as Aarthi reached her hand in for one of them. "See how Aarthi eats, you also want to be strong like her."

I smiled politely, and reluctantly took the last *vada*, soaking it in the remaining chutney that had turned into an unrecognizable mixture between tomato and coconut. Just as I finished the last bite, the doorbell rang. A flock of invisible birds invaded the room.

"*Vaanga!*" Devi shouted, beckoning him to come to the room where we all sat eating.

I liked being around his family and getting to know them, but I was so nervous the entire time. I just wanted to relax and let my guard down for a while. And it would be fun to go shopping. I smiled up at him nervously, not wanting to show too much affection and potentially ruin things.

"Shy like a Tamil girl, *aa*?" Devi teased.

I looked down, unsure of what to say.

"Ready, Jurnee?"

"Sure, of course," I said as I stood wearing jeans and a red fitted T-shirt. I knew that the purpose of this excursion was not to allow us time together, but rather for me to buy a more suitable wardrobe for my time here.

We turned and waved as we walked out of the room and then made our way outside.

"You know I'm afraid of motorcycles," I said as he handed me the helmet.

"But if you have a helmet, you don't have to be afraid."

I rolled my eyes as I fastened it over my head. I hated the tightness of it and that it messed up my hair, but motorcycles were dangerous and Indian roads were chaotic. I'd rather have messy hair than my brains strewn across the road.

I sat behind him, careful to have a bit of distance, before we set off on the narrow street of twists and turns. Everyone turned to look at me. Some mouths opened in surprise. Did they know him? I was getting used to the staring by now, but this staring was slightly different than normal. They stared as if they knew him and were confused.

I tried to dispel the thoughts from my mind and enjoy the warm breeze on my face despite it being December. We passed a woman selling jasmine flower chains, and I was immediately transported back to Kumbalam's Annual Day. The smell was intoxicating and I was certain that she must have the best job in the world.

It was a city, but it felt like a village. There were stark differences between Madurai and Trivandrum. I loved my time in Trivandrum, but it had a totally different vibe. Here in Madurai, so many people were wearing traditional clothing. I saw more local shops rather than chains. It just felt smaller, more personal. I quickly made myself stop making comparisons as I had very limited experience in both cities. I'd been in Trivandrum for just a few days, and in Madurai for not even a full day. I was hardly an expert on either.

Before long, we reached a mall. It didn't feel so villagey anymore. As we made our way inside after paying the parking fee, the many levels made it feel like the Mall of America.

"It's *huge*," I whispered to him as he laughed at me.

Before we could go all the way inside, we were stopped by security. I found it rather odd. Women to one side, and men to another. He went under a metal detector, then held his arms out as they wanded him. I was directed to go into a small room with a curtain covered opening where a woman was waiting for me with a wand.

"Madam," she said as she gestured for me to hold my arms out to be wanded. "London, *aa*?" she asked curiously.

"*Illa*," I said in my limited Tamil. "America."

"Super," she said with an approving nod.

After being approved for entry into the mall, I walked out of the room and joined Anooj on the other side.

"What was that?" I asked him. "It's like airport security just for a mall."

"It is normal only," he confirmed.

Turning the corner, we saw a giant sign: RELIANCE TRENDS. It said that it was four floors and had clothing, household items, and everything else you could ever want. I was amazed by the sheer size of it as we walked inside.

Immediately upon entering was a baggage check, run by a man in a security guard uniform. But then inside it appeared like any other mall store that I would find back home. Rows and rows of brightly colored shirts and dresses hung on display, leggings in a thousand colors sat carefully folded in rainbow order.

As I stood taking in this endless shop, no less than three employees came to see if I needed any help. I felt bad saying no, but I wanted to take the chance to explore on my own for a bit.

I went one by one down the racks of long shirts. Back home, they would be dresses, but here they were referred to as *churidars*, *kurtis*, and *anarkalis*. They came in every color and every style. Some were simple, some seemed traditional, some had sequins and buttons to make them fancier. I was shocked by the prices, though, they were closer to American rates. I calculated the 1200 rupee price tag to about $15. Anytime I'd gone to other shops, things were very affordable. Was that because I'd mostly been in a village? Or a state to state thing? Or maybe because I was in a mall in a major city.

"Do you like any?" Anooj asked me as I began my second round around the store.

"I do, just wanted to see everything here before making any decisions," I replied as I grabbed a white and yellow colored *churidar* from the rack.

I also found a two-toned blue *churidar* that I liked and a black and gold one with a tie around the waist.

The fitting rooms were the same as in America, but the shop employees were much more intrusive. When I'd worked retail in high school, I remembered that rule of having to greet everyone and ask periodically if they're finding everything okay, but here it was that times one hundred, even while I was in the fitting room.

"Madam, everything is fitting okay?" one asked.

A few minutes later, another came, "Madam, need any different size?"

They were extremely helpful; I just didn't need help at that present moment. Each time, I politely declined their offers.

Having successfully selected three *churidars*, I was ready to check out, but Anooj stopped me. "That's all you're getting?"

"Yeah, I've only come for a few days. Why buy so many?"

"But you need more than just the *churidar*, you'll want leggings and *dupatta* to match. Or if you want any simple bangles or earrings, etc., they are here also."

I had a lot to learn about Indian fashion.

There were more leggings than I had seen in my life. Different colors, different lengths, different cuts, different patterns. All of them were as smooth as butter, though. I selected all standard American cuts of leggings, fitted and simple, and went to try them on to make sure that they fit.

They fit differently than American leggings. They were quite long, and the bottom, just above my ankle, had a lot of extra fabric. This time when the girl came to check on me in the room, I accepted her help.

"Can you look at this?" I asked her through the door.

"Of course, Madam. What is the problem?" she asked as she entered the room.

"I didn't notice any petite-sized leggings, do you know which ones will be shorter? These are too long for me."

"Madam, this is the style only. We wear like this," she said as she pulled the material out of the fold that I had made, and arranged it into a bunch.

I looked down at her leggings and, sure enough, they were long like these also. "Thank you," I called as she nodded and left the room. Looking at the tags on the other two, I didn't think it was necessary to try them on as well since they were all the same size and cut, just different colors.

I walked out and met Anooj, ready to face the *dupattas*. *Dupattas* made me nervous. Somehow, you had to have a piece of fabric hang perfectly and symmetrically, and I had no idea how they did it. The older girls at St. Joseph's had done it flawlessly. They pinned it firmly, but yet it looked as though it were hanging loose. They were so talented.

Standing at the rack of *dupattas*, I was overwhelmed. "Should they match the legging color?" I asked Anooj, completely unsure of what I was meant to buy.

"I don't know," he said as I looked around at the advertisements and shoppers to see what was normal.

"You've lived here your entire life, how have you never noticed?" I was mildly annoyed but mostly shocked at his inattention to such a common thing. He must have seen hundreds a day.

He shrugged as he waved over a shop attendant.

"Sir?" she asked as she approached us.

"What color *dupatta* should this be?" he asked her. I was starting to get a bit of sensory overload from everything, so I was glad that he took the lead on this one.

"Madam," she turned to me. "You want to match *dupatta* to legging color. Very simple."

I thanked her as we picked up the three *dupattas* and headed to the checkout. Since I had spent more than 5000 rupees, I was eligible to receive a set of pots. "Do you want them?" I asked him, knowing that there was no way they would fit in my luggage and that my parents didn't need any more pots.

"I'll just call my mom and see. One second." Sometimes I felt like I knew Tamil and that I was improving a lot, but then when I actually listened to people speaking, I was very much aware of how little I knew. In about five minutes, I caught precisely three words – *venum, illa,* and *seri*.

Leaving the pots behind, I was relieved that we were done shopping and secretly hoping to go out and have some *chaat* or something, but we pulled up to another shop. This one wasn't a mall. It was huge and looked very fancy. Above the huge glass windows read SARAVANA STORES.

It was a massive shop, and all the employees wore matching *sarees*. I was immediately intimidated as we made our way to the floor with the *churidars*. Here, they all came in matching sets so at least I didn't have the trouble of finding leggings and *dupatta*.

"Overwhelmed?" he asked, probably having noticed that my mouth was agape. The rows were endless, and I was flabbergasted.

"How can one store sell so many things?" I asked him. We could have easily walked down the aisles for days and not even seen everything. And this was just one floor!

The wall across from me had a giant portrait of a woman I recognized to be Amy Jackson, the British actress who often appeared in Tamil movies. I always wondered why she often portrayed Indian women when there were thousands of talented women who were actually Indian that could play the roles nicely. She was beautiful, though, as she sat beaming in a gorgeous saree.

"You look exactly like her," a salesgirl said as she came up behind me.

"You're too kind," I said with a laugh. "She is much more beautiful than me."

She smiled and said something to Anooj in Tamil. It seemed to be the basic shop dialogue of letting her know if we need help finding anything.

A beautiful green *churidar* with leaf details and Christmas red leggings sat in front of me with a printed *dupatta*. Luckily, it was one of the stiff ones so I could just pin it over my shoulder instead of worrying about it being symmetrical in the front. It was perfect.

Reaching the fitting room, I tried on the poorly fitted *churidar* and sent a panicked message to Anooj. *It doesn't fit. This is like a green potato sack.*

Relax, da, he replied immediately. *Everything is like that. It will be stitched later, this is just the basic model.*

Indian clothes were so complicated. I guess it fit fine then. It even had tiny sleeve bits stitched into the side hem. Why were readymade clothes so uncommon?

"Can we go?" I asked as soon as I saw him. "I can't shop anymore right now; it's way harder here than it is back home." I was beginning to feel claustrophobic and could feel my cheeks reddening.

"Of course," he said gently as we made our way to the checkout table. It was a huge counter with several attendants, each looking at me closely.

"How will we get it stitched?" I asked him nervously. "Your mom and sister know people, right?"

"Of course," he confirmed again. He was always so understanding. I didn't deserve him.

"Madam," the attendant greeted me. "Found everything well?"

"Yes, thank you," I replied with a smile even though I was desperate to leave.

"Do you need any stitching done?"

I looked to Anooj to see if we could just get it done there instead. He nodded in approval, so the attendant made a note on the receipt and pointed us to a woman sitting beside a sewing machine on the other side of the counter.

She immediately stood to greet us, "Stitching, *aa*?" she asked with a warm smile.

I nodded as I handed the *churidar* to her.

"You're looking exactly like Amy Jackson," she said as she nodded towards another giant portrait of her on the wall.

I thanked her, knowing that there was no point in refuting it. Apparently this was a common thought, even though I really didn't see the resemblance at all.

She quickly did some basic measurements and asked how long I wanted the sleeves to be. Within just a few minutes, she had already finished. It was incredibly fast. I had four new outfits and could not wait to wear them.

"Hungry?" he asked as we made our way outside back to the motorcycle.

"Starving," I said with a smile. I was always hungry when I was in India. I wished food back home was this good.

"What do you want to have?"

"*Mirchi!*" I exclaimed without hesitation.

"Are you sure that you're American? You love Indian food so much."

"How can I not? It's just so tasty."

"*Loosu*," he teased me as we approached the *mirchi* stand. I immediately remembered the rules he taught me about how to know if street food was safe to eat. As long as there was a line you would know if it was fresh, if it was prepared hygienically, and if people trusted them. But,unfortunately, sometimes having a long line meant having to suffer through smelling something heavenly while a dozen people stood between you and absolute ecstasy.

It was just as delicious as I had remembered. Spicy, crunchy, soft. I wanted to eat it forever.

"Coconut water?" he asked pointing to another stand a few yards away.

"How can I say no?" I joked. But inside, I had a tiny pang of sadness remembering the bus driver Nehemiah climbing the coconut tree with the school bus, remembering my student Sajith's dad sharing all the fruits on their property. I couldn't wait to see them when I went back next week. It felt like a lifetime since I'd last seen them.

Watching the woman cut open the coconut was incredible. How strong she must be to knock the top off it. It was almost hypnotic, and I watched her cut them off for the other customers one by one.

After finishing shopping and snacks, it was time to go back. I was torn between being happy to get to spend time with everyone again and continuing getting to know them, after all, they were going to be my family. But on the other side, I was also worried about the continued interview.

Back on the bike, bags sitting between us, I meekly held his shoulders, afraid of the judgement of a society of which I did not belong or know the rules. I needed to behave cautiously.

The warm air blew through my hair as I took in the sights around me. The man pushing a vegetable cart up the road, a yellow *auto* swerving through traffic, a giant truck with people sitting in the back on their way to work. Or maybe on the way home. Motorcycles seemingly outnumbering cars, tiny shops scattered around the road and hundreds of pedestrians. It was like "Where's Waldo" had come to life, and there was something happening in every square inch. My senses were overwhelmed in the best possible way. I had missed India.

Arriving back at Devi's house, Anooj's mother was there. She wasn't tall, but she had warm eyes and a shy smile with her hair tied back in a bun and wearing a simple *saree*. She seemed to be friendly, but I was too afraid to find out for sure.

We hadn't even spoken before and, with my rudimentary Tamil, I wasn't quite sure when we would be able to. She seemed to be just as nervous as I was, and we both watched each other carefully, unsure of how to greet the other without being able to verbally communicate. It was like being with Sajith's mom, but with a thousand times as much pressure. One wrong move and she could veto everything.

A couple of times she tried to say something in Tamil, but it was too fast and I didn't quite catch it. A couple of times I tried to say something in Tamil, but the pronunciation was so butchered that she couldn't quite catch it. I wanted her to like me, but I was so nervous that I probably looked like a bumbling fool.

Throughout lunch, I mostly sat in silence while they all chatted amongst themselves. I felt mildly uncomfortable, but it was just like at the hostel – just because I was there didn't mean that I should disrupt their lives. And anyway, it was a good incentive to work on my Tamil more when I got home. I didn't understand most of what they said, but I did catch *irukku, illa, aamaa, aanaal, athanaal,* and some other extremely common words. With each one I recognized, I had a tiny surge of excitement.

"Jurnee," Devi said suddenly as she looked to me. "After two days is your *Poo Vaikkum* function so our *chithi* will come soon to check your blouse."

My blouse? Was I going to get to wear a *saree* again? "Sure!" I couldn't even hide my enthusiasm, which seemed to amuse them.

"*Saree pidikkumaa?*" Anooj's mother said, asking if I liked *sarees*.

"*Aamaa, romba pidikkum,*" I replied affirmatively. I noticed then that I had a tendency to hold my breath after I said something in Tamil because I was so nervous about if they would understand or not.

She smiled. I had said something understandable. Tiny victory. Or should I say, *vetri*.

Soon after, just as they had said, a woman came to the house with a blouse, a notebook, and a measuring tape. She smiled shyly at me as she chatted with Anooj's mom and sister, and she carefully checked the fit. She made notes, waited for me to change and return the blouse, then left just as quickly as she had come. I was so excited to have another *saree* to add to my collection, I just wondered what it looked like.

One thing I really liked about spending time in India was that if you were at home, it was expected that you would have a nap after lunch. Anooj and his mother left, but for us it was lights off, air conditioning on, TV playing a Tamil-dubbed 90s Hollywood movie for Aarthi. It was the perfect equation for a good nap.

That evening, Anooj texted me. *I miss you.*

I miss you, too. I replied. *When can we go out again?*

Tomorrow we'll go to Meenakshi Temple, but it is not good to go out much before marriage, so it may be difficult until we go to Kerala.

In a new city where I only really truly know one person, I couldn't even meet him. I tried to focus on the overall goal of this trip. *Jurnee. You are here to get to know his family, not to spend time with him. You have your entire lives to spend time together. It will be fine.* The sane part of my brain really came in handy sometimes.

Jurnee?

Ya, I'm here, I replied.

Everyone really likes you. I'll pick you up in the morning. Don't forget to wear Indian clothes to go to the temple.

They liked me and I was going to get to wear one of my new *churidars*. This was the best possible news. I decided to wear the green one that had been custom stitched since it was a little bit nicer. I counted down to when we would get to spend some time together alone.

CHAPTER 7

When I woke up, Anooj and his mother had come to the house. I washed my hair, since I'd been instructed to take a *head bath* to go to the temple, and dressed myself in the new *churidar*. As expected, the *dupatta* took a few tries to get it pinned perfectly, but the pants were not quite what I had been expecting.

They were very tight until the knee, then extremely large, then secured with a drawstring at the top. My calves were so tight that it was actually very uncomfortable. When I sat on the floor to have breakfast, everyone could hear stitches breaking and looked at me concerned. I was mortified.

"Pants tight," I said to the group, trying to keep it simple for the different levels of English comprehension.

"*Paravaala,*" Anooj's mother said as she silently instructed me to follow her to the spare room. There, she inspected the rips around my knees and made the disappointed tsking sound that all mothers make around the world.

She pointed to my suitcase, as though to ask if I had alternative pants. Holding up my new leggings and jeans, she pointed to the black leggings – more suitable than brown leggings, yellow leggings, and blue jeans.

She then removed some of her bangles and instructed me to wear them, perhaps to make me fit in better. She found a bindi sticker from one of the shelves and placed it firmly between my eyebrows and smiled approvingly at my braided hair. She reminded me a lot of Sajith's mom and, in that moment, I felt like everything would be okay.

The red pants had definitely looked better since it matched the red details on the *churidar*, but the black leggings were still met with nods of approval when we got back to the bedroom to meet everyone else.

"One minute," Devi called as she got up and opened a nearby cabinet. "Wear these," she instructed me as she passed a pair of beautiful earrings to me. They were small and golden, with a blueish green gem in the middle. "These will match your *Poo Vaikkum* dress also. Keep them with you."

I thanked her as I removed my simple pearls to put the new earrings in, but they weren't normal earrings. I was perplexed by the screws in the back.

"Screws help prevent theft," Anooj said, noticing my confusion.

"Why would they be stolen?"

"Real gold earrings always have screws for security and so they don't fall out," he said.

I'd never worn real gold. Were the bangles real gold also? I tried to press the earring through to the other side of my earlobe, but it was too thick – the screws. Putting my thumb behind the opening and pressing further, I was finally able to make it through the other side as I screwed the back on. It ached slightly but wasn't overly painful. The right side was a little bit tighter, but I was able to still make it through ok.

A mixture of nods of approval and *super*s flooded the room. It was time to go to Meenakshi Temple.

The roads up to the temple were small and packed close together with tight turns. I wondered if this was normal in cities, or just a specialty of Madurai. Turning to park the motorcycle near a group of gold shops, Anooj turned suddenly to go inside of one.

What is he doing going into a gold store? Are we buying something? I wondered. Maybe we were going to get engaged now.

He approached the counter despite a small group already sitting in front of the counter. It was a small shop with an L shaped counter and a few chairs. It was about the size of a big closet. Looking around, I noticed that every shop had the same layout. And they were all also gold shops. I wondered how they got customers being similar shops all within such a close proximity, but my curiosity of what Anooj was doing overpowered my confusion about the shop's business model.

Anooj spoke quickly to the shopkeeper in Tamil, and it seemed that they knew each other quite well. Before I knew it, he was giving the motorcycle helmet and his *cell phone* to the shopkeeper. Why?

He turned to me and asked for my phone also.

"Why?" I said, guarding my phone.

"He's a family friend. You can't bring phones in the temple."

What if I got lost and couldn't find him and no one knew English and I had no way of finding this tiny shop in the midst of a hundred other similar tiny shops? The worried thoughts swirled as I reluctantly handed my phone over, making note that I had to stay very close to him so I wouldn't be stranded. I didn't even know his phone number by heart because it was so long. I didn't know Devi's address or his address. I guess I could message him on Facebook from someone's phone. *Baby Jesus, don't let me get lost*, I silently begged as we stepped back into the narrow street.

A little bit down the lane, we reached a small enclosure just outside the temple where they were collecting shoes. *We weren't allowed shoes either?* I mean, it made sense. But I felt very alone without my shoes and phone.

To make things worse, Anooj and I were separated. There were separate lines for men and women again. And the men's line was moving much more quickly. I was going to be stuck alone, just as I had feared.

After making it through the long line, the stares, and the private wanding, I finally reached the end. I looked in every direction, hoping to spot Anooj, when I saw him standing and waving from the corner. I had never felt so relieved.

I hadn't expected metal dividers amidst the ancient carvings. Nor had I expected such delicate and colorful paintings to be adorning every surface, even the ceiling. With each turn, I expected the color to be faded, but it was fresh and bright everywhere. I wondered how often they repainted it to keep it looking nice. We walked down a corridor where I spotted a giant placard that read HINDUS ONLY.

"Why Hindus only?" I asked Anooj.

"It is a very holy spot, so they want to make sure that proper respect is given. Some who don't believe may just go to look at it, and it would make the line very long for those who really want to go."

It made sense, but it still didn't seem fair. I shrugged and we continued down the path. There was a short table with some ghee lamps. It reminded me of the table I'd seen in Catholic church where people lit the tealights.

"Is this for prayers?" I asked him.

"How did you know?"

"Catholics and Hindus must be more similar than we realized." I replied.

He smiled, "Do you want to light one then?"

I nodded affirmatively as he led the way to another nearby table managed by an older woman. She looked very kind and wore a cotton saree with an elaborate pattern.

"You're so beautiful in Indian dress," she beamed at me.

"*Nandri*," I replied politely to thank her in Tamil.

She turned to Anooj shocked, "*Avangalukku Thamizh theriyumaa?*"

He confirmed that I did know a little bit of Tamil, and they chatted for a moment as he purchased the small lamps. She folded her hands to bid farewell, and Anooj and I made our way back to the lamp table to light them.

"She's so nice," I told him.

"Everyone is nice when you're a foreigner speaking Tamil and wearing traditional dress," he teased.

"Do you have a match?" I asked him, wondering how we could light them.

"No need. Just hold it to another lamp and the flame will transfer."

It was the most obvious solution that I had completely overlooked. We said our prayers and continued walking down the long corridor.

A group of white people sat on the stairs singing *bhajans.* Everyone stared at them. I noticed people staring at me less when I wore Indian clothes and made note to wear them as much as possible to blend in a bit better. It was so freeing to not be stared at constantly.

A man stood with a cart of food like the people in the road. "They sell food here?" I asked Anooj hopefully.

"It isn't food. It's *prasadam,*" he corrected me.

"But I'm hungry," I whined.

"Sure, what do you want?"

"That one," I pointed at something I'd never seen before, but for some reason it looked like it tasted really good. It was just a simple light brown mostly flattened ball.

He ordered my mystery snack and some kind of rice packed in a leaf for himself as we walked to sit in the shade outside.

"What is this called?" I asked, holding up my *prasadam.*

I didn't understand what he said. I really needed to learn more words and sounds to get a better grasp. Not wanting to ask again and look foolish, I smiled and began eating.

It was much oiler than I had anticipated, but it was delicious nonetheless. His rice was a reddish-brown color, apparently due to tamarind. I tried a little bit, but it was slightly sour and not nearly as good as mine.

"Can we go to the temple center?" I asked again.

"You are not Hindu," he insisted. "They won't allow."

"Fine," I shrugged, disappointedly.

As we began walking again, I saw a small museum. "We'll go?" I asked.

"Sure," he confirmed as we walked to the door.

"Foreigner, *aa*?" the doorman asked.

Anooj said something in Tamil that seemed to be conveying that we were getting married soon, so I wasn't a tourist anymore to pay tourist rates.

"She can have discount when she has Indian passport," he said, staring at me sternly.

"I guess it's fair," I shrugged as we paid and walked inside.

"It isn't, though," he argued. "We're getting married soon, and you shouldn't have to pay these inflated rates the rest of your life."

I didn't see it as a huge deal, but I nodded in agreement as we walked down the rows and rows of statues. It was truly never ending. No wonder this place was so famous, it should be one of the seven wonders. I only wished that I could take photos.

The museum wasn't as crowded, and it was quite cool and damp compared to the heat we'd been suffering when we sat outside the temple to eat. It was a welcome break from the sauna-like climate that I hadn't yet adjusted to. I read that in May the heat would be even worse and shuddered to think how I would manage.

"Ready?" he asked as we reached the end of the rows.

No, I thought. "Sure," I said. I wasn't ready to give up these tiny prized moments alone with him without the pressure of trying to gain acceptance.

"What's wrong?" he asked, seeing the torn expression in my eyes.

"I just like being alone with you. You know how nervous I am being around new people and trying to make them like me when I'm absolutely terrified and fixated on making sure they don't change their minds."

He began to laugh.

"Why are you laughing?" I said angrily.

"Because there isn't anything to worry about. They've already said yes. The *Poo Vaikkum* function is soon. This is just a formality. I've told them everything about you, and they're completely fine with our marriage."

"Are you sure?"

"Don't think so much," he teased me. I wanted to hug him so badly, but I knew it was deeply frowned upon for several reasons: being in India, being unmarried, being a foreigner, being in a temple. The list was endless.

We walked out together, collecting our shoes, and made our way to the gold shop. This time, there were no customers, so we sat while Anooj chatted with him for a while. Unable to communicate and having been without my phone for a couple of hours, I took the chance to catch up on my notifications.

Nothing new, just a couple of messages from friends and worried messages from my parents.

Everything is fine, I replied. *Things are just really busy. I'll talk to you soon.*

Be safe! my mother warned.

There was absolutely nothing to be worried about. I didn't ever even leave the house alone.

By the time I got bored scrolling through my phone, they had finished, and we found his motorcycle to go home.

When we arrived, Anooj was given two plastic buckets. One was full of dried red chilis, and the other full of a mixture of dried leaves and red chilis.

"Come," he instructed me as we walked outside again.

"Where are we going?"

"To get powder."

"You don't buy it?"

He laughed and continued walking. Eventually we reached a small, loud house.

There were three blue and grey machines, a scale, and a woman dressed in a beautiful *saree* despite the dust and spice powder in the air.

Anooj spoke to her in Tamil as she weighed the buckets and put them in two of the machines. The back part fed into the front where she monitored it and helped some of the pieces go down into the grinder. After several minutes, the powder had fallen back into the bucket. I thought it was finished, but she poured it again into the back of the machine for a second pass.

After they were finished with the second pass, she poured them evenly on an old rice bag.

I looked at Anooj, confused.

"It has to cool off before we can put it in the bucket. It is extremely hot from the machine right now."

I'd never even thought about where the spice powder came from. Life was just so different here, and I was completely in love with everything.

The next morning, it was time for the *Poo Vaikkum* function, and I had no idea what it involved or what it meant, just that it had to do with getting engaged.

The day started like normal, waking up on the floor of the family bedroom. I was instructed to take a *head bath* again, despite having taken one yesterday. It was supposed to be done on all auspicious occasions.

As I sat on the bed of the second bedroom drying my hair, the most gorgeous *saree* I'd ever seen was laid out before me. It was a mixture of green and blue and changed color with a tilt of the fabric. It was reminiscent of a peacock, and the blouse had beautiful gold and pink embellishments to lend a nice contrast. It was absolutely stunning.

"*Pidichirukka?*" Anooj's Chithi said to ask if I like it.

"*Romba pidikkum,*" I confirmed. I couldn't believe that she had stitched the blouse herself. Even the embroidery. I was blown away by her talent.

We shared a silent smile like before, unsure of how to communicate due to the language barrier. Devi came to the room with another dress. "First, you will wear this," she proclaimed, as she and Anooj's *chithi* went to the other bedroom with my new *saree*. My heart sank. When would I wear the saree?

I was left with a bubblegum pink *churidar* with matching pants and a matching long overcoat. These kinds of outfits were much easier to assemble than sarees, but for some reason, I still loved sarees immensely and longed for the day I would learn to wear one without assistance.

As I pulled it over my head and looked at myself in the mirror to put on a bit of eyeliner and mascara, I was hardly recognizable. Gone was my long hair openly hanging down my arms and back. It was tied into a proper braid, with a small dot placed carefully between my eyebrows. Real gold earrings sat in my ears, my earlobes still mildly aching from the thick posts. I didn't even wear a watch at home and rarely bracelets because they were uncomfortable to wear while using a computer, but now I stood with numerous bangles tinkling on my wrists. I felt like a completely different person.

Emerging from the bedroom, I saw several people that I had not seen before, and I instantly felt my face redden. Unsure of what to do, I smiled and walked quickly to the other bedroom, hoping to find a familiar face.

There in the corner was Aarthi. *Phew.* "*Aththai!*" she called out. "Dress super."

"Yours also," I said with a smile. Devi had coordinated our outfits so that we would both be wearing pink and the peacock color. Her dress was gorgeous and even had a matching headband.

Devi came to the room clutching a long strand of jasmine that she pinned into my hair. After a small adjustment and a knowing smile, she nodded to indicate that I should follow her to the living room to meet the guests.

I was led to a white plastic chair against the wall. The whole room, about fifteen people, were watching me carefully. Maybe because I was a foreigner, maybe because my face was bright red from nervousness, maybe because they knew that I was to marry their relative. Or maybe a mix of everything.

To my surprise, after just a few minutes, I was led back to the bedroom. All the ladies followed, and the men remained seated in the living room.

Blouse and underskirt in hand, I was led to the attached bathroom to change. What had been the purpose of wearing the *churidar* for just a few minutes? A wave of panic washed over me. Was I supposed to wear this in front of all the women in the bedroom? I felt extremely uncomfortable knowing that I would soon be standing half covered in front of my boyfriend's female relatives, most of whom I had met just moments earlier.

I walked into the bedroom, arms crossed and hunched over, as I tried to hide my stomach. The women looked to each other confused, and I had a brief flashback of standing before Nissy Miss as she declared how funny it was for a foreigner to be shy. Maybe they shared the same sentiment.

Devi and another girl came to my side and began to tuck the *saree* in around the skirt. While she made the pleats at my waist, the other girl began making the shoulder pleats and arranging the *pallu* which was to hang over my left shoulder. It took only a couple of minutes for them to finish. I was astonished.

As I looked in the mirror, Devi adjusted the jasmine again and smiled. It was much longer than the normal jasmine chains that I saw, and I wondered if there were different lengths depending on the occasion.

Anooj's mother gave an approving smile and gestured for me to have a seat on the bed. Everyone was staring at me. I stared at the floor, unsure of whose eyes to meet.

The girl who pleated my *pallu* sat beside me. "Are you excited about getting married?" she asked.

"Mostly terrified," I joked.

"I totally understand. Actually, this is my first event that I am attending as a married girl, I married Anooj's cousin last month. I'm Uma."

"Congratulations! Is he in the living room with the others?"

"No, he's in Canada now. Do you want to see photos?"

I nodded as she showed me hundreds of their wedding photos in the most beautiful outfits I'd ever seen. Every photo looked like a movie poster, and I suddenly couldn't wait for it to be my turn. I couldn't help but to wonder how I would look at our wedding, what I would wear.

"So when will you join him in Canada?" I asked.

"As soon as I pass the IELTS exam," she said worriedly.

"When is it?"

"After two months."

"Definitely, you'll pass," I smiled.

She smiled back, unconvinced.

"There's no way you won't. Your English is perfect," I said encouragingly.

She nodded, wearing the same uncertain smile.

"Jurnee, it is time. Come," Devi called from the door as everyone stood.

This was it. I was going to go in front of everyone, and I had no idea what was happening, and Anooj was nowhere to be seen, and what if I messed up and did something wrong and then they changed their minds and then everything was ruined. My mind began to spiral out of control as my cheeks reddened and my eyes became warm.

I caught precisely three tears falling as all the women in the room looked at me, shocked.

"Do you not want to get married?" Uma asked me.

"I do, just nervous about being in front of so many people."

She turned to the women and translated my dilemma. Turning back to me, she began, "Jurnee, this is nothing. There will be a hundred times more people at the wedding itself. Be cool."

I remembered my students in the hostel using the same phrase and that I would see them soon. I remembered that this was all for Anooj, and I would see him soon as well. I remembered that these people were soon to be my family, and I needn't be nervous around them, but I couldn't help it.

His mother and sister each took one of my hands as we emerged from the bedroom and into the living room. They led me to a red plastic chair in the center of the room, and everyone stared at me. I stared at the floor, again unsure of where to look. Afraid that the panic and nervousness would overwhelm me and make me cry in front of everyone.

Anooj came through the door, and I couldn't help but to smile. He wore a dark blue button-up shirt and khakis. Why didn't he wear Indian clothes to match me? The Indian in American clothes and the American in Indian clothes, how the tables had turned. *Jurnee, no. No affection. You read about this. Divert your attention, don't mess this up.* I looked down.

One by one, the guests came to give me leaves and wipe powder on my face. I didn't know what to do, so I held the leaves and smiled at them one by one.

The leaves contained a mixture of money and small foil packets. I didn't know the significance or meaning of any of it, just that it must have some ancient traditional meaning and I should enjoy this moment, because based on forums I had read online, it was not common for Indian families to accept a foreigner, and I was extremely lucky. Not one person seemed dismayed or even mildly upset about it.

After everyone had passed by with leaves and powder, it was time to eat. The chairs were moved, and a woman swept the floor before putting down banana leaves. I was again reminded of Kerala and couldn't wait to see them.

In the middle was a heaping pile of rice, with several tiny scoops of vegetables surrounding it. A metal cup of water sat in front of the leaf, and a paper cup of what I recognized to be *payasam* sat beside it. I'd had payasam once at Sajith's house and loved it. The milky sweet noodles had been surprisingly delicious.

Without a spoon, I decided to try to eat with my hand to blend in a bit better and within moments, every eye was on me again. Or had their eyes even left to begin with? Probably not.

"You look so beautiful in *saree*," Anooj whispered to me, careful to not be overtly noticeable.

"Why didn't you wear Indian clothes?" I asked him softly.

"*Chumma*," he said, the Tamil way to say *just because.* "Everyone really likes you," he continued softly.

"Are you sure?" I was still surprised by how easily I had been accepted.

"They say you are very shy and cute like a Tamil girl."

I had to be careful to maintain my composure and not mess up. I was *this* close to the finish line. Even though he said there was nothing to worry about, there was everything to worry about.

After everyone left, I immediately went to the second room, switched on the fan, and laid down. I didn't mind that I was fully dressed in my *saree*, jasmine, and borrowed jewelry; I was exhausted.

Over the next few days, we settled into a routine, and I became less nervous. Everyone was totally fine with us. Even extended family.

Devi rolled over beside me, "Happy Christmas," she said.

"Aththai! It's Christmas!" Aarthi squealed with joy.

"Last night I made a crib for you," Devi said cheerfully.

A crib? I smiled despite my confusion as her husband leapt from the bed to lead the way for the three of us to see the crib she had made.

There on the table in the living room was a nativity scene. It wasn't a set like we have back home. She had *made* it. There was the main structure, the tiny manger, all the people and animals, hay scattered everywhere, an angel. There were even twinkling lights wrapped around it all. It was incredible.

"You did this?" I asked, shocked. "It's beautiful."

"This is your home now. You celebrate our festivals with us, we celebrate your festivals with you."

"Do you like it?" Aarthi asked enthusiastically.

"I love it."

"Lot of time she spent," her husband said.

Embarrassed to speak my broken Tamil in the midst of such a display of effort and talent, I resorted to English. "Thank you," I said to her, taking her hand in mine.

I would never hold hands with someone back home. But here it was very common to show platonic affection physically, just not romantically. I had learned it in the hostel and often found myself wishing that people back home felt more open to be affectionate with each other. There was so much societal pressure to keep distance and maintain this stern independent persona. But what was so wrong with needing each other? Was it bad to be interdependent?

She smiled and squeezed my hand as we sat for breakfast. Her husband had brought the spinach *vada* complete with an array of chutneys. We had had cinnamon rolls every year on Christmas morning for as long as I could remember, and now I was having *vada*.

"I'll just go and come," I said, remembering the local dialect as I excused myself to the second room to call my parents. It was Christmas Eve evening back home, and they'd be going to church soon. Luckily, calls were free through WhatsApp.

"Jurnee? How are you! Is it Christmas there? Merry Christmas!" my parents exclaimed in a jumble of excitement.

"Merry Christmas!" I replied. "Going to church soon?"

"Just waiting for your mother to finish getting ready," my father replied. "You know we always like to be first in line for the good candles," he joked. They were all exactly the same, but he always insisted that they were different.

We chatted for a few minutes until my mom had finished getting ready and they had to go to church. "We'll call you in the morning!" my mom shouted. "Merry Christmas, Jurnee. We miss you."

"Love you guys."

"We love you, too."

I wondered what Christmas here would be like. I wondered if they knew about the real Christmas, or just the secular part. They had a nativity scene instead of a Christmas tree so they must have some background in it.

Just then, Devi knocked on the door. "Jurnee? Open, open, we have a surprise for you."

"What is it?" I asked, confused. I was already so surprised.

"Here we always wear new dress for festivals. This is a new *saree* for you."

It was stunning. And heavy. Beads were stitched over every border of the blouse and even the *saree* itself. It was red for Christmas and absolutely stunning. But very, very heavy.

"Take bath and come. I will dress you."

I now had two new *sarees*. And a new family. This was the best trip ever. *Well*, I thought. *Until the wedding. That will probably be even better.*

I looked at myself in the mirror as she finished draping the *saree* for me. The beads glinted in the light, and I felt invincible.

"Red color is super for you," she said with a wink.

"Thank you for choosing it," I smiled to her. She had impeccable taste.

The only other *sarees* that I'd worn had been very soft and lightweight, maybe a kind of silk, but this one was so heavy. Even my prom dresses hadn't been this heavy. As I walked across the floor, the beads scratched my ankles, but I didn't mind. After all, they always say *beauty is pain*.

When Anooj arrived, he was wearing a T-shirt and sweatpants.

"Really?" I hissed at him, dressed in a brand-new saree with gold jewelry and jasmine again.

"How was I supposed to know that you would be so dressed up like this?" he asked, laughing at my disappointment in his wardrobe selection.

"Go home and change," I demanded.

"I can't," he insisted, despite everyone else being dressed nicely - his mother, his sister, her family, me.

We spent the day watching movies, and for dinner they surprised me with pizza, an American classic. We finished the evening by lighting sparklers that they had left over from *Diwali*.

It was unlike any other Christmas I'd experienced, but somehow the best one yet. I was a little disappointed that he still hadn't proposed and wondered when it would be.

Day by day, I felt more connected to my new family. I felt bad for being so shy and hesitant with them at first, but I appreciated them so much and all that they did to make me feel more at home. I just wished that they liked me as much as I liked them. I was unsure of how to make any grand gestures, being the outsider of the group.

After the new year, it was time to go back to Kerala to see everyone.

It was in that moment that I realized that the magic husband leaf from the temple priest had worked its magic in just ten months. Sajith's father really knew what he was talking about.

CHAPTER 8

Anooj came to the house at six to start the trip. It was six hours away, and we would be back home by evening. Tomorrow was my last full day, and I wasn't ready to go home.

Dressed in one of my new *churidars*, we set off for Kumbalam with their portion of the chocolates. As we got into the car, he showed me a giant bag *full* of snacks. Apparently, his mother had packed them for us. Snacks and solitude, what more could you ask for?

The topography slowly changed from clusters of houses, to highway, to greenery. We were driving through a forest with winding roads, and it was stunning, but I immediately felt sick.

"Please pull over," I said frantically. I hadn't been carsick in years, maybe it was the altitude mixed with winding roads. He stopped immediately and waited.

Luckily, a little further up the road was a pharmacy, also known as a *chemist*. He went in and emerged a few minutes later with a small brown bag containing just a few tablets. "Eat them," he said, weirdly forcefully.

"I need water."

"You diva foreigners," he teased as I rolled my eyes. He immediately went to another shop to bring a bottle of water.

Opening the car door, he smiled a mischievous smile. "Do you want the left hand or the right hand?" he asked.

"The hand with water," I said.

"But something is in the other hand too," he said with a smirk as I tried to peer behind his back. He turned quickly to hide, "First choose."

I looked at him with widened eyes, silently urging him to show both hands. He had gotten water and a Dairy Milk. I was ecstatic.

"Do you want to drive?" he asked.

"I'm sick, how can I drive? And besides, you have manual cars here. I can't drive them."

"Yes, you can, it'll make you feel better to be driving. Come try."

I sat hesitantly in the driver's seat as I was suddenly made aware of the oddness of having three pedals at my feet, and only two feet with which to press them. Quite the conundrum.

"Press the two left pedals and turn the key," he said as I followed instructions.

It turned on, that was a good sign at least.

"Now, continue pressing both and change the gear to first," he continued.

An awful sound came. It was like an angry raccoon with emphysema. I couldn't get the gear to change, it wouldn't accept it.

More people were coming near the car, peering inside, silently judging me. "I can't do this," I said to him as I unbuckled my seatbelt.

"Yes, you can," he said reassuringly.

My heart was beating alarmingly fast. My face red, my palms sweaty. I tried one last time, eyes closed in a silent prayer when they should have been open and looking at the gears. But against all odds, it went to the correct slot.

"You've got it. Press both feet down all the way and try again to change the gear."

To my surprise, it worked.

"Now keep your foot pressed on the left one and move the brake foot to the accelerator and slowly apply pressure."

I held my breath as I followed his directions.

The car began to fall down the slope. *No no no no no no no,* this wasn't happening. We were going to die or, at the very least, someone else on this hill would. Luckily, my foot instinctively knew where the brake was, but now a string of lights lit up on the dashboard.

"Trade me sides," I demanded.

"No. You can do this," he insisted.

"I'm going to break your car."

"I have insurance."

"I'm going to ruin your transmission."

"I'll buy a new one."

"I might run over someone."

"There's a hospital nearby."

"Please, Anooj. I can't drive manual," I said, tears in my eyes.

"You can. You also felt such about being selected for the job, remember? Have faith in yourself, you can do anything you put your mind to."

He always knew exactly what to say, but now a car was behind me. *If this car slides back any further, I'm going to hit them,* I worried.

"Go back," I shouted to the driver behind me.

They looked confused.

"Reverse drive!" I tried to say in more universal terminology.

Still met with confusion.

"Reverse or I will hit you!" I shouted again, hoping they would realize the urgency of the situation. I hadn't even gone a foot forward; I didn't want to roll backwards into a car.

"Hit me, *aa*?" he said as he got out of the car.

Oh no. Oh no. Oh no. I realized that he thought I meant that I would physically assault him, not that this car would hit his car. I turned to Anooj, grimacing. Would he be able to get us out of this like he had done with the unruly *auto* driver at Kovalam Beach?

He saw my panic and turned to Anooj. After a moment of tense-sounding Tamil, they were laughing. Everything was fine as the driver waved and walked back to his car.

"What happened?"

"Don't tell someone that you're going to hit them, *loosu*," he teased me.

I cringed. "Oops."

When I noticed the car behind had given us some space, I decided to try again despite the small crowd that had gathered around us.

Feet on the left and center. Keys turned. Gear shifted. *So far so good.* I looked to Anooj for confirmation as I began the final step, switching the brake foot to the accelerator.

It was a delicate balance, lifting one whilst pressing the other down, but I made it. Sure, there were noises and bumps and extremely judgmental stares, but I did it. I moved forward.

"See, Jurnee. Perfect," he said as cars behind us honked angrily, going five miles per hour in first gear.

After everyone had passed us, I decided that I had proved enough. "Okay, your turn."

"What, *my turn?*" he asked. "This is your lesson only."

"I had the lesson. Please, now drive. We'll never reach if we go like this."

Realizing that I was right, he nodded and I pulled to the side. I didn't press the pedals correctly and the lights came again on the panel as the car jerked to a halt. *Oops.* I shrugged as I got out of the car and sat in the passenger seat with a sweet sigh of relief. I was free.

Anooj gently tapped my arm, "Wake up. Come," he insisted as I looked outside to the small hill in front of us with a train track on top.

Groggily, I opened my eyes, mildly annoyed, and followed him out of the car and up the narrow stairs on the side of the track. The higher up we went, the more beautiful it was. We could see for miles, and the greenery was truly majestic.

"How did you find this place?" I asked, curiously.

"Just wanted to find a place that was high enough to see everything," he replied as he lowered himself to one knee.

Was this it? Were we getting engaged? I wasn't even cute. I had just woken up.

"Jurnee Eleanor Ryan, I love you more than anything in this life. You complete me and make me better in every way. Will you marry me?"

He reached into his pocket and pulled out a box. Within it sat a thick golden band with a round diamond placed atop. It was reminiscent of some of the more feminine styles of class rings in high school, but much more beautiful.

I couldn't get the words out to accept, so I had to nod vigorously as he put his arm around me and the ring on my right hand.

"It's the left one," I whispered.

He blushed as he rectified his mistake.

I stood in his armpit for several minutes as we took in the scenery around us. It had been perfect. We were engaged now. This was it. It was unbelievable. I took out my phone and noted our location. *Thenmali*. We would have to come back some day.

"I love you, Jurnee," he whispered as he held me a little tighter. "More than you'll ever know."

Suddenly, a man in a *lungi* and dirty white tank top emerged from the tunnel shouting.

Anooj turned quickly, taking my hand in his and running down the stairs. The ring box fell to the rocks as we hurried to the car.

"What happened?" I asked, worried.

"We aren't supposed to be there, he was threatening us if we don't leave immediately."

And just like that, our magic moment had ended.

When we arrived at the school, it looked exactly the same. The same security guard sat at the post behind the fence to let us in. The same flagpole to the side where we hoisted it for Annual Day. The same regal building with giant pillars stood tall in front of us, and I remembered how breathtaking the view from the roof had been. It seemed like yesterday, but somehow also like it had been in a different lifetime.

Memories came flooding back as Anooj parked the car in front of the school. Children ran in every direction, surrounding us. I bent down to hug each one tightly, trying not to cry.

"Jurnee Miss! You came!" they exclaimed.

"Of course, how can I not come back?"

My heart ached a bit not seeing Deepa, Sajith, or Vivek. They had finished tenth standard and were now in a different facility. Devu ran to my side. "Jurnee Miss, come fastly!" she said as she pulled me across the lawn, running.

I looked back at Anooj helplessly, hoping he could manage on his own. He waved reassuringly as I ran in the stampede of children led by Devu, who quickly reached for the chocolates I was holding.

Teachers waved, amused, as we ran past them. I hoped to catch up with them soon, but I was curious about what Devu had in store.

She led me to the kitchen where Cook Auntie was standing in a beautiful teal *saree* with silver sequins. I ran to her with a hug, "*Sundhari*," I whispered, Malayalam for *beautiful.*

She held me tightly as I breathed in her warmth. She was exactly how I remembered her.

The crowd around us began to grow as I was pulled in a hundred directions.

"Jurnee Miss!" Radhika exclaimed. "What is this?" she asked as she grabbed my hand.

Gasps through the crowd spread like wildfire.

"You got married without us?" she asked, hurt in her voice.

"We're getting married and wanted to invite you all!"

"You and who?"

I forgot that they didn't know him. He'd only come to Annual Day. I began to point when I saw him walking closer. "That boy," I said happily.

"Jurnee Miss! A Malayali! Suuuper!" Devu said cheerfully.

"Actually, he is from Madurai," I corrected her.

"Super! Happy Wedding!"

"You'll come, won't you? It's just a few hours journey."

"Cannot. We are in school."

"It will be in May," I said, hoping she would change her mind.

"Call my father. He will tell."

I confirmed the number that I had saved in my phone from before and made a note to call him later.

Hopefully, they would be able to come. I loved Devu and her brother, their whole family had been so welcoming when I stayed with them in Varkala.

As Anooj grew closer, the whispers grew louder. By the time he reached us, everyone knew who he was and what he was doing here.

They all chatted with him, hanging on his every word. He was a celebrity to them. I sat and watched, cast aside as chopped liver, with the exception of Solomon, the youngest of the hostel, who kept turning my ring from side to side to watch the light reflect off the diamond. He was in first grade now and starting to lose his baby face.

Ananya Miss came through the doors suddenly, "Jurnee Miss! Welcome home!" she called as we ran to meet each other in a hug. "I've missed you so much!" she exclaimed.

"I have, too! How have you been? It's been so long!" we chatted on WhatsApp sometimes, but it was hardly the same as it had been when I was here.

"You're getting married?" she asked, but it was more of an exclamation. "To an Indian! How exciting!"

I smiled coyly. I was just getting married, and everyone was acting like I'd just won the Super Bowl or something, it wasn't *that* big of an accomplishment.

"Oh! I forgot," she started with a quick pat of disappointment on her head. "Everyone come back to school. MD Sir says we mustn't miss class."

Groans spread across the room. "*Vaa*," she demanded as they begrudgingly followed. Anooj and I followed along as well.

The students went to their classrooms, but all the teachers were in the office. Nissy Miss welcomed me with open arms in the most literal sense of the phrase. "Jurnee! You've returned! And what's this about you getting married!" In a hushed voice, she turned and asked, "Is it him?"

"Yes," I smiled shyly. "He is Anooj."

"He's looking so handsome. Super pair," she said with a smile. "But one doubt."

"What is it?"

"Isn't he the boy from Annual Day? Were you in love that time?"

"Just friends then."

She looked at me suspiciously but nodded with approval. Anooj smiled as some of the teachers began to chat with him in Malayalam. Everyone loved him and promised that they would try to come, but the time was passing by too quickly, and I knew that soon it would all be over again.

We had only been there for a couple of hours when the buses began to gather at the back of the building. It was time for them to go home. It was almost time for us to go home, too. I'd been looking forward to seeing them for months, and the time I was actually with them passed by in the blink of an eye. At least I'd see them again in May.

"Jurnee!" Joseph called as he emerged from his office. "How are your parents? Congratulations on your marriage!"

"They're doing well. Thank you, sir. We hope you can come!"

"I will do my best to come," he confirmed. I was so happy that everyone was going to try to come, and I couldn't wait to see everyone in fancy wedding clothes like another Annual Day. I was a bit sad to be missing it, but hopefully I could see it next year. At the very least, I would see photos all over Facebook.

We chatted for a bit before we realized that we had to leave. We would barely make it home before midnight now, but I didn't want to leave them. This wasn't my second home, this *was* my home. I loved them like my family and caught myself beginning to cry again as we reached the car.

"Please stay longer," Devu called out, pulling my hand.

"I wish I could, but my flight home is tomorrow."

"Come soon Jurnee Miss," Nandu demanded.

"I will," I promised as I hugged them tightly and hoped desperately that they would come for the wedding. We pulled away slowly, and I waved to my students and colleagues with a smile on my face as tears silently fell.

"Do you want to call your parents later to tell them we're engaged?" Anooj asked.

"Not really. I'd rather share it with them in person," I said as he reached to hold my hand. We were getting married and had just invited people. After all that had happened a couple of months ago, I never thought that this day would come. It was indescribable.

When we got back to Madurai, he dropped me to Devi's house, and I slept the sad kind of sleep when you know that it is your last day somewhere. I wished we could at least stay in the same house, but that wasn't how it was here.

The next morning, he came early to pick me up, and we spent the day exploring Madurai a bit more. We did some shopping for my family and bought a farewell gift for Aarthi since she had been so sweet during my visit.

I surprised myself how much I liked his family. I'd been so worried that they wouldn't like me, and I was realizing now how foolish that had been. They were even sweet enough to realize how much we would miss each other and encouraged us to stay out all day.

That evening was hard. I wanted to be excited that the next time I saw him, we would be getting married. But I was devastated leaving him again. Long-distance relationships were so hard, and I couldn't wait to one day live together, hopefully soon. It broke my heart to have to fly home without him.

"Jurnee," he said encouragingly as we reached the airport. "Don't be so sad every time. We will be married in a few months. This time next year, we will be living together, and you will think it was silly being so upset to leave me for a few months. You'll be wishing that you could take leave from me," he joked.

I laughed while I cried. "But we don't even know which continent we'll be living on."

"After we've both visited each other's homes, we can make a clear decision."

He was always so logical. "I'm going to miss you," I sniffled as we took my bags out of the car and began walking towards the airport entry.

"I'll miss you too, *payanam*."

"What is that?"

"You are a Tamil *ponnu* now. I can't call you *yaathra*. I have to call you now *payanam*."

I was forever amazed that he knew so many languages. I barely knew a handful of sentences in Tamil, but he could have full conversations in so many different languages. He was absolutely inhumanly perfect, and I adored him.

We continued hugging tightly. Me trying not to cry, him trying to tease me so I would stop crying. We were the perfect blend.

"Madam, enough," the guard shouted at me. I guess he was the airport police *and* the hug police.

Anooj and I stared into each other's eyes, wishing we had just a little more time.

"I love you, Jurnee," he whispered.

"I love you, too," I said with one last squeeze as I turned to walk into the airport.

"Sorry, madam. I didn't realize," the guard said as he gestured to my ring.

I turned back to Anooj one last time and waved. I took a deep breath of Madurai air and walked into the airport. I wasn't ready to go home yet.

CHAPTER 9

I was so excited to tell everyone that we were engaged, but I had to wait until my parents knew. And I had to wait to tell them until I got home. It was almost a three-hour bus ride to arrive.

I couldn't stop turning my ring in the light. I didn't even like diamonds, but it was like a tiny rainbow laser on my hand, all of the colors streaming out of it at all different angles. I remembered back to an article I'd read in school about how humans liked shiny things because it was an instinct to make us attracted to water and thought about what a Neanderthal I was.

It was almost five when I got home, and I knew my parents would be home any minute, so I ran upstairs to freshen up.

When I heard the door close, I ran downstairs. It was my mom.

"Oh, honey!" she exclaimed as she hugged me tightly. "You're home!"

But her excitement quickly turned to anger. "How long have you been home? Why didn't you call? I'd have come sooner!"

"I only came like five minutes ago, relax," I teased her as my dad walked through the door as well.

"Jurnee! Come here!" he scooped me up in a bear hug like we hadn't seen each other in years.

"I wasn't gone for that long, guys," I said with a mischievous grin.

"It was too long! You know how we miss you when you're gone."

"I have something to tell you," I said somberly as I stepped away from the hug.

They looked to each other with a knowing smile. There was no point in announcing it, they already knew what was going to happen.

"Anooj and I are engaged!" I said with a squeal as my mother took my left hand to inspect the ring, turning it side to side to see the diamond glinting in the light.

"Congratulations, Jurnee Dhakshinamurthy," my father said formally.

"It will be Jurnee Anooj, actually," I corrected him.

They looked confused. "What?" they demanded in unison.

"Your last name is your husband or father's first name in Tamil Nadu."

They looked to each other with a bit of concern, almost like I was joining a cult.

"But, Jurnee, dear," my mom started with a concerned tone. I thought she was going to bring up some valid concern like if was even legal to change my last name to a first name, but it wasn't. "How will we address cards to both of you? Should we write Anooj Dhakshinamurthy and Jurnee Anooj? Mr. and Mrs. Anooj Dhakshinamurthy? Just Anooj and Jurnee?"

I tried to not laugh at such a silly issue. "Just write Jurnee Anooj Dhakshinamurthy. Everything will be covered that way."

She nodded but didn't seem fully assured.

"Great idea," my dad chipped in, still confused but trying to be supportive.

"Let's order pizza!" my mom suggested. It was the perfect celebration meal.

Over pizza, I told them all about my adventures during the past two weeks. I told them about how huge the Meenakshi Temple was. I told them about seeing my students again. I told them about meeting Anooj's family. I told them about our Christmas celebrations and the *Poo Vaikkum* function.

They were mesmerized and completely lost in my stories. Whenever I talked to people about my experiences, I was usually met with this. They couldn't imagine a life so different that their reactions were almost as though I were telling them a movie plot. It made me feel so disconnected.

So much had changed in this past year from living in Kumbalam to being in a long-distance relationship, and I just felt like I didn't totally fit in anymore. My experiences were so vastly different than those of my family and friends that I felt almost a decreased connection with them. Not purposely, but there had been a subtle shift in values and opinions. My parents were still perplexed about why I took my shoes off in the house now. It had grown to be habit.

When I got up to my room, I did what any freshly engaged girl would do and posted about it online. Just a picture of the ring, a picture of us, and a picture of the train track.

Not a minute later, my phone rang. "Jurnee! What is this!" Marina shouted.

"What do you mean?" I had just posted, it couldn't be about our engagement already.

"You're engaged! I can't believe it! I'm coming now!" and she hung up. The current generation was really bad at phone etiquette.

Anooj must still be asleep, I thought as I texted him. *Marina coming over, will call after.* Just so that he wouldn't think I was ignoring him when he woke up.

I had tried to sleep on the plane and in the bus to avoid jetlag since I had to go to work tomorrow, but I was starting to feel extremely tired. *Just two more hours, Jurnee*, I thought to myself as I got up to splash some water on my face. *Stay awake just for a bit longer.*

Marina and Krista came together and attacked me with hugs, oohs and ahs, as they turned my left-hand side to side in wonder. I was the first of our friend group to be engaged, apart from Sharlie, who got engaged during college, and Karen.

"Don't forget about us after you get married!" Krista exclaimed.

"I could never," I said as I hugged them tightly.

"Are you so excited? Do you know when it'll be yet?"

"May 15!"

"Of this year?" they asked, concerned.

"Yeah. Of course."

Marina backed up slowly, "Are you pregnant?"

I couldn't help but to laugh. "No, definitely not."

"Suuure?" she asked inquisitively with a lifted brow.

"Positive," I laughed. "Long engagements aren't common there."

We spent the next hour going over the details of the engagement when I caught myself slipping in and out of sleep. Jet lag struck again.

"Get some rest, Jurnee. We'll see you soon," Krista said with a hug as they both got up and walked to the door.

"We love you," Marina said.

"Goodnight, guys," I said as they turned off the light and I rolled over to sleep.

The next morning at work wasn't quite as supportive. Sitting in the teacher's lounge for lunch, a few colleagues came to inspect the ring. They offered cautionary congratulations.

"I don't think this marriage will work," one said bluntly. This was precisely the second time that we had ever spoken, and I couldn't help but to wonder what exactly she was basing this assumption on.

"Have you even met him? Are you just trying to get famous on *90 Day Fiancé* or something?" another asked.

I regretted telling them but didn't want to ruffle any feathers in my new job, so I kept silent.

One teacher who was normally quiet came to my side, "I'm very happy for you," she said, uncharacteristically loud, to be sure the others heard her.

The first commenter who had been rather blunt came again, "But what if he just wants to marry her to move the US and then harvests her kidneys for a new iPhone? I heard they do that."

The quiet teacher and I looked to each other and rolled our eyes.

"I'm Bridget," she introduced herself. I recognized her from our new teacher orientation.

It wasn't a big school, but we were always busy with our students, and I usually had my nose in a book during lunch, so I hadn't really spoken to most of the teachers outside of meetings. They were pretty nice, for the most part, but most were older than me and had families, so there was hardly time to really get to know each other.

"I'm Jurnee," I said with a smile.

"It's nice to see you again! When are you getting married?" she asked.

"May 15! I'm so excited!"

"This May?" she seemed taken aback.

"My fiancé is Indian, and they often have short engagements," I explained.

"Wow, that's so cool. Have you been to India?"

I told her all about my two trips to India. About the village, my students, and all of the things that happened. Almost drowning, seeing the biggest stars I'd ever seen, attending church where I didn't understand a single word. About our engagement and the *Poo Vaikkum* function.

"That's like a movie! What an incredible experience!"

"I miss it every day."

"Are you two going to live here or there after you get married?" she asked.

We had discussed it a lot, but never formally decided. Living in the US would provide more opportunity and would be easier to for him to adapt than me, but we both loved India. "We're still thinking about it," I admitted.

"You're so lucky to get to *choose* where you want to live! I can›t even imagine ever leaving Illinois. Everyone I know is here."

"Even I," I said, catching myself fall into my occasionally Indian patterns of speech. "Me too," I corrected myself.

She smiled as the bell rang. "See you tomorrow!" she chirped as she closed her lunchbox and walked towards the door.

I had finally made an office friend.

That night, the wedding excitement continued as Devi woke up early to send me pictures of *lehengas*. They were basically a fancy crop top with a full skirt and more decorative *dupatta*.

She sent me two options, one was ocean blue with a pink *dupatta*, and one was teal green with a reddish orange *dupatta*. It was no contest. The blue one was my favorite shade.

One thing struck me as strange, though. The boy who worked at the shop was wearing them. Why not just lay them down to take a photo?

The blue one! I sent her, excited to be picking out wedding clothes. It was getting so close, but it was a little bit alarming how little planning I was involved in.

I had been asked what some dishes I liked were for the catering, color preferences for dresses, and wording ideas for the invitation... but apart from that, I hadn't been involved even a little.

"I feel bad making them do all of the planning," I said to Anooj in a call later that night. "Shouldn't I be more involved?"

"This is normal, don't worry so much. They are so happy to be planning it, you should see them running here and there like busy bees," he chuckled.

I couldn't help but to smile. After how worried we were about them liking me and approving our marriage, I was so relieved to know that they were as excited as we were.

"So what will the wedding be like?" I didn't want to be caught off guard like I'd been at the *Poo Vaikkum* function and start crying again in front of everyone.

"Just some rituals. They will tell us what to do at that time, no need to worry about it now."

"But I need to know," I insisted. My anxiety did not welcome surprises, especially not surprises in front of hundreds of guests.

"Okay, so there will be a small fire that we walk around. There will be a reception for clicking photos. There will be a big feast with the banana leaves. During most of it, we will be sitting, so there isn't a lot of work."

"How long will it be?"

"Maybe two or three days?"

"Like seventy-two hours of marriage?" I asked, shocked.

"No, just one function a day. Functions will be a few hours long, not full day."

That was a relief at least. I was used to American weddings with a twenty-minute ceremony followed by a three- or four-hour reception.

"How many different sets of clothes will I need?" I asked, half-jokingly and half-genuinely curious. With all the events, surely, I would have a new outfit for each.

"Probably five." He said it without even a hint of amusement. I was going to have five wedding dresses for three events. Hopefully they weren't expensive.

"And how many wedding dresses will you have?" I teased him, knowing that, in India, any article of clothing was called a dress.

"I don't know. My mom will tell me."

He had it so easy.

"I forgot to tell you, my mom sent me some *saree* pictures for you. Just tell me which you like," he said as my phone vibrated several times.

"But I thought I was having a lehenga?" I wondered.

"That will be for the reception. This is for the marriage itself."

The photos were stunning. The *sarees* were mostly gold with a bit of red detail. They were extremely intricate, and I couldn't imagine how much time and effort had gone into designing and weaving them. They were all extraordinary, and I didn't know how I could choose just one. I wanted all of them, but they looked expensive.

Some had red leaves, flowers, paisley designs, or just diamond shapes tucked between the gold details. "I like the one with big red flowers," I said as I sent him one of the photos back to confirm.

"These ones are the two most important, so they will take your opinion, the others will be a surprise."

"Wait, that's it? Don't I get to see the rest of it?"

"It's a *saree*," he said like that was supposed to mean something to me.

"Yeah, but it's six yards of fabric, and I only saw one square of it."

"Wedding *sarees* are nine yards, but it will look the same throughout. Don›t worry."

"What about the blouse?"

"They will sort it for you, my *chithi* knows stitching. Remember?"

"You know that I need to know this, Anooj. This is extremely stressful, especially not having any part in it. For us, usually it is the bride who plans everything, and I don't know what we'll wear, what we'll be doing. I don't know anything about our own wedding."

"You know the reception dress, the marriage dress, the invitation, what we'll be eating. Those are the main things."

I guess he was right, and it was a huge help for my anxiety to not have to plan a huge event for hundreds of people. Maybe this was for the best. Just sit back and enjoy instead of worrying about every detail. *But that's you*, I laughed to myself. India brought out a more outgoing side of me, but I was still the same anxious mess either way.

"How are your Tamil classes? *Sollu*," he said, compelling me to say something in Tamil.

"*Enakku eppadi Thamizhla paesu theriyaadhu*," I joked, telling him in horrific grammar that I didn't know how to speak in Tamil.

"Try *pannu*," he urged.

"*Muyarchi*," I corrected him. I at least knew the word for *try*.

"Why do you always want to say every word in Tamil?" he asked. "Some words we will say in English only, don't bother to learn them."

"But if I'm speaking Tamil, I want to speak only in Tamil. Why do you want to say English words when you're speaking Tamil? It doesn't make sense. Say *muyarchi*. Say *aluvalagam*. Say *mugavari*."

"Learn more common words, don't waste time on these," he pleaded with me. But he was pleading on deaf ears. If I was going to learn Tamil, I was going to learn it all the way.

"*Ellaam kathuppaen.*" I said, telling him that I would indeed learn everything.

"Hopeless," he teased.

"*Illa, neenga dhaan,*" I replied, pointing the *hopeless* back at him.

Most of my Tamil was riddled with errors, and I was nervous to speak it, but small simple phrases weren't too bad. I really hoped that one day I would achieve full fluency to be able to speak with his family properly, but the more I learned Tamil, the more difficult I realized that it was.

"So, who all is coming?" he asked, changing the subject.

"My parents, obviously. Krista and Marina probably. I met a new girl at work, she seems nice and might come."

"Anyone else?"

"I'm not *that* close to many people who would be willing to fly so far and spend so much."

"Once they get here, there won't be any expenses though, let them know that."

"What about their hotels and all?"

"Traditionally, we pay for guests' hotels, and for travel expenses of people who are very close."

"Isn't that expensive?" I was shocked. That was such a huge expense, especially for such a big wedding.

"It's part of it, not a big deal. But they won't have to pay for anything once they get here."

That was definitely a good selling point. I made a note to ask them again this weekend and see how it went. They still hadn't given me a definite yes or no, and I was starting to worry.

"Jurnee?" he asked softly.

"What happened?"

"I'm really happy we're getting married."

"Me too." Even with all the stress of getting married in just five months, knowing that I was doing it with him made it so much less stressful. It was just a few days, and then we would be together our whole lives. The sliver of me that dreaded the wedding because I would have to be in front of people was overshadowed by how badly I wanted to be in the same country forever.

"If you get tensed or anything, call me anytime. You know I'll stop everything for you."

That was probably my favorite thing about him. No matter how ridiculous my stress was, he would take the time to help me work through it and relax. He was unlike anyone I'd ever met. "I know," I smiled. "And for you as well."

"You should sleep though."

"But it's so early!" I protested.

"We have to go to deliver the invitations."

"So just drop them off at the post office later. Why do you have to go now?"

"It is not so simple here."

Everything in India was so different and complicated, especially with weddings. I paused, knowing a lengthy explanation was coming.

"We have to hand-deliver every invitation."

"But that is *hundreds!*" He couldn't be serious.

"We have a saying here. In English it's like, *if you mail me an invitation then I will mail you a gift.* It means that if you mail them an invitation then you didn't care enough to take time to give it to their face, so they won't attend."

That seemed a bit dramatic. Maybe they were worried about it getting lost in the mail? I had no idea, but he was hardly the one to voice my concerns to.

"It isn't so bad. My sister and her husband will also deliver some."

"That's good at least."

"Goodnight, Jurnee. I love you. Text me when you wake up."

"Goodnight, Anooj. Love you, too." It was only nine o'clock. This was the worst.

I took advantage of the extra time to text the group chat I had with Marina and Krista. *Guess what! Apparently it's tradition in India that the wedding party pays for your hotel and everything, so once you get to India, you won't have to pay for anything! You just need the visa and the flight and then everything is covered!*

Hopefully that would sway them. I ran downstairs to tell my parents as well.

They weren't in the living room. They weren't in the kitchen. They weren't in their room. "Mom! Dad!" I shouted walking through the house.

"Down here!" they called from the basement.

Out of breath, I panted, "Once ... you get ... to India ... you won't ... have ... any expenses." I really needed to get in shape before the wedding. "Anooj said that it is tradition to pay for the guests' hotel rooms and everything, so you just need the visa and the flight! Isn't that great!"

I was helping pay for the wedding, so the cost scared me a little bit, but who was I to argue with tradition?

"Actually, honey," my dad started hesitantly.

No. I held my breath. What was he going to say? This didn't sound good.

"Your mother and I won't be able to make it to your wedding."

My heart sank to my stomach, and, whilst falling, it shattered into a thousand pieces.

CHAPTER 10

S orry, what?" I asked, unsure if I had heard him correctly.

"We won't be able to make it. We're very sorry."

"But it's my wedding. Literally the most important day of my life." How could it even occur to them for a second to not come? I was absolutely dumbfounded.

"I know this might upset you," *Might? Really?* "But we've looked at all of our options, and it simply isn't possible. We will attend your wedding in America."

"The Indian wedding *is* our wedding," I said, holding back tears as I ran upstairs.

I didn't even have words. My heart felt like someone was literally squeezing it. *They're my parents. How can they not want to come?* Slamming the door behind me, I threw myself onto the bed. How could they do this to me?

I ignored the knock at the door. It became louder and more persistent. "What!" I shouted, more demandingly than questioningly.

"Please listen to us," they pleaded, so I reluctantly opened the door.

They sat on my bed with apologetic faces. I sat stoically, trying not to cry.

"We love you. And we love Anooj, he's a great guy. We just don't think we can travel to India."

"I've gone twice. Why can't you? It's not like we can't afford it."

"That's correct, but it's just a difficult time right now."

"A difficult time, how?" What could *possibly* be difficult? This was my wedding. Their daughter›s wedding. You couldn›t pay me to stay away from my daughter›s wedding.

"You know I'm afraid of flying, Jurnee," my mom said nervously.

"There is medication, therapy, sedation. It's two days of the total trip, and you aren't going to be by yourself." She had to be joking. She'd flown multiple times, but this one was the one she was afraid of?

"I just don't think I can do it."

"And honey," my dad started cautiously. "May is a really busy time at work. There's no way I can get time off."

"Tell them it's your daughter's *wedding*."

"We have deadlines, Jurnee."

"They have the internet, you can work remotely. You're really going to miss my wedding to be with your boss?"

I looked away, betrayed. My own parents weren't coming. How would I explain it to Anooj? To his family? This was an absolute nightmare.

"Can't you have it here instead?"

"His family is huge. Dollars have way more value than *rupees,* and it wouldn't be possible to buy tickets for all of them. And the difficulty of getting all of their visas approved. All you have to do is fill out a two-page questionnaire, and you get a visa in a day. Why can't you see how important this is?" I was going to add, *to me,* but I couldn't speak. The heat behind my eyes and my cheeks spread, and tears flooded out. I was heartbroken.

They walked out of my room and closed the door. I hid under the blankets, praying to wake up from this nightmare.

I immediately texted Anooj, *They aren't coming. I don't know what to do. Everything is ruined.* He was asleep, and there was no way that he was going to reply right away. I had to calm myself down.

I lay in my cocoon of sorrow, hoping that I could fall asleep and all of this would have been a dream.

I got a call suddenly. Krista and Marina three-way video call! Perfect.

"Guys, you'll never believe the day I've had," I started.

"Are you sick?" Krista asked.

"No, just having a day," I laughed in self-pity.

"We just, we have something we needed to say and thought it would be best if we did it together."

"What's up?"

"Well," Marina started hesitantly. "We can't come to your wedding."

I felt myself beginning to shake. Was she serious?

"I just, I can't afford it right now. I'm so sorry."

"As soon as you get there everything is covered, though. Please come."

"Jurnee, the ticket is almost a thousand dollars. There's no way."

"I can help you pay for it. I'm still living at home, so I don't have a lot of expenses."

"I can't ask you to pay for it. I'm really sorry."

"You're not asking, I'm offering."

She paused and Krista started, "Actually, we're afraid to go."

"Why? I've gone twice. It's not haunted or anything."

"We've seen *Slumdog Millionaire*. They pour acid into kids' eyes, and there's so much crime and poverty."

"You trust a movie over my firsthand experiences?" I was shocked.

"We're just scared, Jurnee. And it's so expensive. And the flight is so long. Why not do it in Italy or something if it can't be in America?"

In that moment, I decided to write a book about my trip to Kerala so that even if my own friends and family wouldn't come, at least I could dispel stereotypes for future travelers.

This was the absolute worst thing that could have happened. And it was then that my phone rang. Anooj had finally woken up. I cut the call with Marina and Krista without even saying goodbye.

"Jurnee, what happened? Who isn't coming where?" he asked concerned.

"No one is coming for the wedding," I admitted, tears streaming from my eyes.

"You are coming, right? It cannot happen without you," he teased, trying to make me feel better. But it didn't.

"No one is coming."

"What do you mean? Who?"

"No one. My parents. My friends. No one is coming."

He paused. "Tell me exactly what happened."

I told him everything. All of the excuses and how shattered I was.

"We'll give them a few days to realize how important this is to us, and then we'll ask them again. They'll come, don't worry."

"They won't come," I insisted. "Everything is ruined."

"It isn't ruined. I'll talk to them after a few days, okay? We'll get it sorted."

In just a matter of hours, every single person I cared about shat on me like a car below a tree full of birds. My sadness began to turn to anger. "I don't want them to come if they won't come on their own."

"You don't mean that. These people are all very important to you, and you're important to them. It isn't easy for everyone to make it out to India."

"It's for our *wedding*," I insisted. "How could they not come?"

"I'll sort it out, don't worry. Everything will be fine, *da*."

It didn't feel like everything would be fine. It felt like everything was closing down around me. The most important people in my entire life weren't going to be there on my wedding day Well, wedding *days,* but still. They had to come.

"We'll look in the budget and cut a few things to pay their tickets so that all they need to do is get time off. What about that?"

"Do you think we have enough to spare?"

"I will find it. Or we will add to it. No matter what, we will get them here. Please don't worry."

He always knew how to fix things. He was far more logical than I was.

I was still upset, but a tiny bit of hope manifested. Maybe he could explain it better and they would listen to him. It was worth a try.

"Don't worry. We'll give them a couple of days to think it over and realize that it hurts you, and then I'll ask them again. Don't worry."

He knew that he had to reiterate it because I'm the queen of worrying. I Googled how to say it in Tamil. *Kavalai podu.* I was very much *kavalai podu*-ing.

"Jurnee?"

I realized that I hadn't responded. "Okay."

"This is just the wedding. One tiny thing in our whole life, don't think so much on it. Everything will be fine."

He was right. I couldn't *not* worry, though.

The next couple of days were awful. Trying to avoid everyone because I couldn't bear to face them. Pretending I was fine in front of my students and even to Anooj. The most important day of my life was probably going to come and go without any of my friends or family by my side. Devastated didn't even begin to describe the ache.

"So?" I asked Anooj when he called that night.

"I tried, Jurnee. I'm so sorry."

I lay on my bed and wept like a child. I felt bad knowing that Anooj probably felt helpless in everything. He was trying everything he could to make me feel better, but I was devastated.

If they didn't like him it would have been one thing, but everyone actually really genuinely liked him. They liked his character, they liked how well he treated me, they liked how respectful and kind he was, they liked how happy I was and the changes they'd seen in me while we'd been together. But they wouldn't come.

Because of India? The place that had taught me so much and given me so many opportunities? The place where the people I met were the kindest I'd ever met in my life? The place that I yearned for everyday? They were afraid of it? It made no sense. If I had gone by myself for *months*, they could come in a group for my *wedding*. How was this even an option?

If someone told me that they would pay everything for me, I just needed to get a visa and show up, it wouldn't even be a question to me. I would leap at the opportunity. *Maybe they don't like you as much as you think they do*, the rude part of my brain chipped in.

"I think I'm going to sleep, Anooj."

"Are you sure? We can talk or watch a movie together or just sit in the call if you want."

"Yeah, I need to sleep." It wasn't even noon yet. I slept until the next morning.

The days dragged on. I barely spoke to anyone, even Anooj. Wedding planning didn't excite me. Devi was planning the gift bag for guests, and I tried to pretend that I wasn't apathetic, but I just didn't have the energy for it. Maybe this was all a mistake, and the fact that no one coming was a sign.

"Good morning, *payanam*," he said when I called him.

"Are you busy?"

"I'm never too busy for you. What is it?" My hesitation concerned him, "Are you okay?"

With a deep breath I said, "I don't think we should get married."

"You want to postpone so that more people can come? I can talk to my mom, that should be fine. We'll figure it out."

"No. I mean. I don't think that we should get married. In general."

"We will figure it out. We'll find a way to convince them to come. They don't oppose the marriage, it's just a location issue."

"But I can't do it on my own. At your wedding you're supposed to be surrounded by everyone who loves you and cares about you, and I'll be surrounded by strangers. Your family is so nice and welcoming, but I don't know them that well yet."

"The wedding is just an event. It's the marriage that counts, and you'll be surrounded by people that you love for your entire life. And I love you, Jurnee. You're everything to me. I'll be there with you."

"Only because you have to be," I teased him.

"I will be by your side for our entire lives. And my family really likes their new *marumagal.*"

"Are you sure? You really think we should do this?"

"I *know* that we should do this. We belong together."

Maybe he was right. "Are you sure?" I asked again.

"I'm positive. I love you, Jurnee. Don't give up."

He was right. I did have a flair for being dramatic and letting my anxiety spiral. It was just a wedding; it would be fine. I was still upset, though.

"Let's watch a movie," he suggested.

"Which one?"

"Have you seen *Nadavula Konjam Pakkatha Kaanom?*" he asked.

I couldn't even pronounce it. "Is it Tamil?"

"*Aamaa,*" he confirmed.

"What about?"

"You know Vijay Sethupathi, right? From *96, Pizza, Soodhu Kaavum?*"

"The main guy?"

"Yeah."

"He is good. Is he in this one, too?"

"He gets amnesia on the eve of his marriage. It's very good."

"Happy ending?" I asked. I couldn't handle a sad ending right now, and I knew Tamil movies weren't always guaranteed a happy ending.

"Of course. Do you want to see?"

"Okay, fine. Which site?"

The movie was good, and Vijay Sethupathi was incredible as always. It even had a few funny parts, and I was pleased to know that it was based on a true story of the cinematographer's own marriage.

"Anooj?"

"Jurnee Madam," he teased.

"Don't play with crickets before the wedding."

"How many times should I remind you that cricket is a game not an insect?" he said with a laugh.

"I miss you."

"I miss you, too. Just a few more months, and then we'll be together forever. Don't take tension."

"I know. It's hard, though."

"My family will be here for you. And so will I. We all love you."

"Don't leave me," I said softly.

"You're the one I have to worry about," he joked.

Pulling up to the school several weeks later on a Monday morning, something was different. Out of the corner of my eye, I noticed that the billboard down the street had changed. It changed almost every month. Last month it had been for a local veterinarian; the month before, it had been for an insurance agent.

But now, hundreds of yards away, there it was on a plain sign in huge block letters – JURNEE, THIS IS A SIGN.

He must have called them weeks ago when I said that I needed a sign to get married. All the stress had culminated, and I was second-guessing everything. And there in the clouds was him sending me a sign that it was the right thing to do.

I immediately called him.

"Jurnee? What is it? You never call this time of day. All okay?" he asked, concerned.

"Did you buy a billboard?"

"You said you needed a sign, right? I gave you a sign."

"But how did you afford it? Aren't they expensive?"

"We put aside money to pay for flights remember. There was extra in the budget and if the wedding is cancelled then there is no budget at all. I had to do something."

He was perfect. "I love you, Anooj."

"I love you, too. When is your flight?"

"Thursday after school gets out for the summer."

"I can't wait to see you."

"Me either." Every doubt that I had ever had was washed away in that moment.

That evening, Krista and Marina came over.

"We're really sorry we can't make it," Krista apologized.

You could have if you wanted to, I said silently.

"We'll celebrate after, okay?" Marina asked.

We could have celebrated during, I said snarkily in my head. I loved them, but I was so angry.

"We brought you a gift," Marina said as she passed me a box.

Opening it, I discovered that it had four trinkets inside.

"Something old, something new, something borrowed, and something blue," Krista added. "So, you can bring some of our traditions with you."

There was an old picture of the three of us, a nice camera, a pair of pearl earrings, and a blue robe that said BRIDE.

I couldn't stay mad at them. Sure, I was still very much disappointed, but they were my best friends. "Whose pearl earrings are these, though?"

"My mom's," Marina said. "You know she has a thousand pairs. She's obsessed."

"Thank you, guys," I said, hugging them. I wished they could come. "I'll miss you."

"Take lots of pictures! We want to see everything."

You could have seen if you would have agreed to come, I said in my head, but I smiled instead.

On Thursday as I was packing, my parents came to my room.

"Sweetie, we wanted to give you this as a wedding gift."

I peered up to the door, still heartbroken that they weren't going to come.

"We love you, and we wish we could come."

I tried to smile but couldn't. Of everyone, they should have been the first to say that they wanted to come. "Love you, too," I said quietly.

They handed me a box that contained a very heavy traditional family Bible. It had the places to write your family trees. It looked like grandma's.

"Thanks, guys," I said with a weak smile. It would have been better if they would have come instead.

Looking at the clock, my dad took my suitcase as I swung my backpack over my shoulder. It was time to go.

When we arrived at the airport, everything around me was green and beautiful. The air was soft and fresh like early Chicago summer. Everyone was running here and there in the airport, excited for their vacations, happily walking in groups. And there I was, walking alone to fly alone to get married alone.

How was it possible to be so heartbroken and so excited at the same time?

CHAPTER 11

Landing in India for the third time was surreal. I no longer felt like a foreigner or a tourist, it all felt familiar.

I took a deep breath and instead of the excitement and curiosity that had flooded me on my first two visits, I was now at home. It was like holding your grandmother for the first time after a long gap. I breathed in India's fragrance and held it in, absorbing my surroundings.

The same *vada* man was there. The same jasmine woman was there. Everything was the same, but it was so much hotter now that it wasn't winter. I scanned the crowd by the airport doors, looking for someone familiar. Anooj had said that his friend's parents would pick me up but hadn't told me what they looked like.

Suddenly, I heard someone calling for me, "Jurnee? Jurnee?" a man and woman came to the edge of the gate to confirm that it was me.

I smiled and nodded to confirm, and they immediately hurried to the opening to join me.

"Welcome to India, Jurnee!" they exclaimed in unison. "Did you reach okay? Feeling tired?"

It had been a very long few flights, but it was nine in the morning, and I had to force myself to stay awake all day to get myself on the correct sleeping schedule. It was an arduous task to overcome jetlag, but there was no way around it.

She wrapped her arms around me in the tightest, most sincere and welcoming hug. More heartfelt than hugs I'd received by people I had known my entire life.

She carried with her a small metal plate containing a string of jasmine and one of the invitation cards for the wedding. Her husband went a few yards away to take our photo together as we stood closely with giant smiles.

She offered to put the jasmine in my hair, but I was dirty from the flight. "After *head bath* I will put," I said quietly. *Would I offend her by not putting them immediately?* I wondered. I was in a bad shape after flying for so long and wanted to clean up before adorning myself. I hoped I hadn't hurt her in saying it. There was so much to learn about Anooj's culture and societal expectations. Could I do it all? Western culture had permeated India so much and it wasn't as difficult for him to adjust as it was for me.

He took my bags to load into the car as she sat in the passenger seat, and I got in the back. "How do you like our India?" he asked as he got into the driver's seat and started the car.

"I love it," I said cheerfully as I gazed out the windows. I was home.

"Are you excited to get married?" she asked as she turned to face me.

"Mostly nervous," I joked.

"Don't be nervous. He is a very nice boy, and his family is good also."

I looked down and smiled at how lucky I was for such a welcome, for such amazing in-laws, for Anooj. I had won the lottery without ever buying a single ticket.

We kept driving as the roads became smaller and smaller until we came to a house with a simple gate on a crowded street. There inside the gate stood Devi and a few others that I recognized from the *Poo Vaikkum* function.

Anooj's friend's parents started to get out of the car, so I took off my seatbelt and opened my door to join them.

"No!" shouts came from every direction.

Devi came to my door. "You cannot get down. We will come to my house now," she said as she got in the back seat with me.

Anooj waved to me from inside the gate, but he didn't come out. I had come ten thousand miles, and now he stood just ten feet away, and I couldn't meet him. I tried not to let my disappointment overtake the joys of almost reuniting as Devi started chatted about wedding preparations.

She noticed me looking longingly at the gate, wishing I could go to see Anooj. "You are not allowed to go to the boy's house before marriage," she said firmly but apologetically.

"Why?"

"Tradition," she said with a shrug and a giggle.

There was so much to learn, but after a pause I asked, "What if they are childhood friends? She will have been to the house before."

I could see her thinking about it. "After the alliance is fixed, she will not be allowed to come again until after the marriage," she confirmed.

It was so complicated.

Anooj's friend's parents came back to the car, and they began chatting happily in Tamil with Devi. I sat and looked out the window, wishing I could see Anooj, and counting down the days until our wedding and I would be able to see him. Six more days.

Six more sleeps.

Driving down the winding roads, we reached Devi's house in just a few minutes. I was surprised how fast it was, or maybe I was just too enthralled by everything around me to realize how much time had passed.

We pulled up to the same familiar gate with the patch of land across the street where a dog and a cow were quietly resting. Some neighborhood schoolboys were lighting sparklers without parental supervision, and no one seemed alarmed.

We took off our shoes and carried my bags the short distance into the guest bedroom, and everyone joined in the living room for snacks. Instead of watching them awkwardly or browsing social media, I stared at my feet. I anticipated that there would be a lot of foot-staring these next few days.

Luckily, Aarthi came home at that moment and excitedly pulled me away. Everyone was nice, I was just bored with no one to talk to, and it felt awkward to be sitting with people but not interacting with them.

"How was the journey?" she asked with a giggle.

"Very long," I said with an accidental yawn.

"Want to sleep?"

"No, no. I should try to stay awake to break the jet lag."

"Correct. *Mama* also says," she replied. For a moment I was confused until I remembered that *mama* was *uncle*. Learning Tamil was really coming in handy. I was just too nervous to speak it to anyone because of all my errors.

She pulled out a doll grocery store and we played, shut away in the bedroom with the air conditioner.

"Jurnee!" Devi beckoned.

Not feeling comfortable shouting in someone else's house, I got up to the door, "What happened?" I asked.

"The jeweler has come." She turned and indicated that I should follow.

He sat on the floor, and we all sat around him in a circle as he brought trays of rings. Some were small, thick, and silver. Some were larger, thin, and gold. I wondered what the difference was.

Anooj's brother-in-law noticed my confusion. "Finger ring and toe ring," he confirmed.

I was getting toe rings? Looking around at Devi and Anooj's friend's mom, I noticed that they both wore them also. Theirs were smooth, though, and these had ridges and small colored details. I wondered if there was any difference in the meaning. Would I graduate into the smooth ones after a few years of marriage?

The jeweler sat a tray on the floor with gold rings first. Some had small diamonds, but I felt that my engagement ring already had one so it wasn't really necessary. Some had shapes molded into them. One had a lion, one had a heart, a few had flowers. They were extremely ornate, and I was shocked by the details present. Back home it was just deciding the stone. No one paid a much attention to the metal, but here, the metal *was* the focus. The stone was an afterthought.

I was silently instructed to try them all on to narrow down which fit. Of the dozen left, I settled on a small dainty flower. I wouldn't be able to wear it as a set on my left hand, but that was fine. I still had my right hand.

Now it was time for the toe rings.

They were in an identical tray, but all in pairs. They were all silver, but some were wider than others. Devi advised me to get one on the shorter side. After deciding the widths, then I tried them all on to see which fit.

Finally, we were left with five designs. We settled on the set with ridges that went around and a pink decal on the front. Devi took the wedding ring and toe rings in their boxes, and the jeweler left with a nod.

That was easy. I wondered if Anooj would also have to wear so many rings and symbols of marriage after we got married.

As if on cue, Anooj, his mother, and his *chithi* arrived at the house. Anooj and I smiled at each other from across the room, unable to greet each other openly. The three of them chatted with his friend's parents before they stood to leave.

I regretted not catching their names, but I was sure that I would see them soon. She hugged me and he waved as they went on their way.

Anooj's *chithi* carried with her a shopping bag as she led the three of us into the guest room, leaving Anooj alone. I had no idea what was happening, but I smiled and went along with it.

She pulled out two blouses. One was red and one was blue, and they were the most ornate fabrics I'd ever seen. I didn't even have words. They had jewels stitched onto them, borders, designs, beads. You could barely see the material underneath. And they were heavy.

The red one was to be for my wedding *saree*. The blue one was to be for the *lehenga* at the reception.

I stepped into the bathroom to change into the red one, which was like any other blouse apart from the elaborate details. It clasped in front and fit well. They walked around me slowly, inspecting every seam, and after a few minutes, it was given approval.

I went back into the bathroom to change blouses, but this one was different. Maybe it was *lehenga* style to have a side zipper instead of a front clasp. It was also much longer, which I was thankful for. I'd been shown several *lehenga* photos and asked how much stomach I wanted to show and had been shocked to see some that had been extremely short like a stylish sports bra.

I'd requested it to be much longer, almost meeting the skirt and, thankfully, it seemed that it would. It was perfect, and the color was my favorite shade of blue. I walked into the bedroom, and the inspection continued. This also was met with approval. I wondered if it would have even been possible to fix them in time since the wedding was just a few days away.

"You know, our *chithi* did the stitching," Devi said, gesturing to her aunt.

"She'll be acting as your mother in the marriage also," she added.

"What do you mean?"

"There are rituals that your parents are supposed to do to bless the marriage, so without your parents, we have to have someone to come."

I knew that it was a big deal for my parents to not be here, but I hadn't realized that they played a key role in the wedding itself.

"And no brother or cousin-brother also," she said with a tsk. "Don't worry, we will manage."

I smiled to disguise my devastation. It had hit me again that I would not have my family or friends at the wedding. I would be alone.

"Can you dye your hair black?" she asked suddenly.

I looked down at my light brown hair with flecks of red in it. "Why?"

"To match our hair extensions," she said as she held up a two-foot-long black braid. "We have black henna you can dye your hair; it will wash out after some time."

I looked at my hair again. I had never dyed it, never permed it, rarely even used heat on it. I couldn't just *dye* it to match extensions. Couldn't they dye the extensions to match my hair? But then they would be unusable by anyone else, so I guess that was out of the question.

She saw my hesitation. "It will wash out, *pa*. Don't mind it."

I didn't want to say no, but I definitely didn't want to dye my hair. I smiled, neither agreeing nor disagreeing, and made a note to speak to Anooj on it. Maybe he could help me refuse politely.

She handed me the skirt to try on with the *lehenga* blouse. The inspection continued, and it was given approval by all. Just as I'd expected, the blouse and skirt met perfectly.

"So, when is the hair and makeup demo?" I asked, excited to see how I would look for the wedding.

"Demo means?" she asked.

"Like, before your wedding they will show you how it will look so that you can make sure you like it."

"You will like it, no need."

"But we always have them. In case you want to make any changes."

"She is my friend, she will do it correctly."

No demo, and I might have to dye my hair. I took a deep breath and tried not to panic. And my family isn't here. And my friends aren't here. And I can't even really speak with Anooj. My mind started to spiral, and I tried to focus on breathing while the three of them stared at me.

"Okay," I said, trying to smile. It was just a few days of events. It was hardly something to argue about or to get upset about. *Let it be,* I said to myself. *You will drown if you fight the current; it's a new culture and a new family, take in the new experience and don't force your way.*

After carefully folding the blouses, we made our way back to the living room to join Anooj.

"What about the cake tasting?" I asked. It must be coming up soon.

"What cake?"

My heart sank. This really was going to be a completely different experience, wasn't it? I shook my head and tried to move on, but Anooj caught my eye and smiled with a small nod. Did that mean that he was going to help me get a cake? Or just that he was empathizing with my plight?

Maybe I was just getting upset because I was exhausted. It *was* way past my time to sleep back home.

Just then, Naren came with lunch, and they all chatted amongst themselves. I heard *kalyaanam* frequently, so

I knew they were talking about the wedding. I silently ate my okra curry and wondered what the next few days would hold. Would I be able to do it?

That night, I woke up at one. I had gone to sleep at ten, a normal sleeping hour, but for some reason, I couldn't stay asleep. I looked around at the dark room where everyone else slept peacefully.

I stared at the ceiling, willing myself to sleep. I tried counting backwards. I was tired, why couldn't I sleep?

Are you awake? I texted Anooj.

"Last seen 11:05 pm" his WhatsApp banner read. He was asleep. A few congratulatory messages waited for me on Facebook, but I disregarded them.

Was it not contradictory to congratulate me while simultaneously not attend my wedding? I went back to staring at the ceiling, spiraling in my thoughts and silently weeping. I was exhausted, but I couldn't sleep. I was surrounded by people but felt alone. I desperately wanted to see Anooj but couldn't. It was just days before my own wedding, and I had never felt so miserable. Everything was so different from the wedding I had been dreaming of since childhood.

Snap out of it, I scolded myself. *You love Anooj. It's just your wedding, not your marriage. This is a few days' event compared to your lifetime together, don't fixate on it. Everyone loves him and they love you, they just couldn't attend.*

I ignored my sane advice and continued staring at the ceiling, tears silently falling into my ears.

Just then, Devi rolled over and saw me. *"Ennachu, pa?"* she asked worriedly.

"Nothing, just tired."

"No, something is wrong. What happened?"

"I'm not getting sleep, and I'm nervous about the wedding, and I miss my family, and I'm just very tensed," I squeaked out, trying simultaneously not to cry and also not to wake up anyone else.

She came closer to me and cradled my head on her lap, combing her fingers gently through my hair as I silently wept. "We are your family. Don't take tension. We all care for you a lot."

I didn't remember falling asleep, but I slept late, and it was the first time I'd slept more than three hours since I'd arrived. The next afternoon, I had the worst headache from crying.

"*Aththai* get ready, we will go soon," Aarthi said excitedly.

I tried to feign excitement, "Where to?"

"Surprise," she said, barely able to contain herself.

I smiled and went to get ready.

We arrived at a busy plaza with several shops. As we all got out of the car, Anooj and his mom also joined us, and we walked towards a small fancy shop. It had glass windows, and I held my breath while I read the sign. It was a cake shop.

I looked at Anooj, almost in tears from my excitement, and he nodded as if to say that it was no big deal. But it was a huge deal.

It felt like a parallel universe in that I was getting married to the most incredible man I'd ever met, but the details were all completely different than anything I'd ever seen. Nothing was what I had expected and none of my family was here, but now I had this tiny raft of familiarity to hang onto. We were going to have a cake tasting.

The employee didn't quite understand what a cake tasting was, so instead, the six of us ordered a slice of several flavors and ranked them. Since my Tamil wasn't good, I wasn't involved in most of the conversation, but I did give preference to the classic chocolate and vanilla.

We decided to order a three-tier cake, but they labelled it as a ten-kilogram cake. As in almost twenty pounds? Did we order the right thing? How much do cakes weigh?

We decided to get the bottom two tiers in vanilla, and the top in chocolate, which had a surcharge of five hundred rupees since chocolate was deemed a "specialty flavor." Strange.

Looking through binders of designs, we saw ornate ones, cutesy cartoon ones, plain ones, romantic ones with hearts everywhere, some with flowers all over them. We settled on one with butterflies and placed the order to be delivered at our reception.

We were getting married in just a few days. Tomorrow was my *marudhaani*, better known as henna back home. The day after was the reception, and then it would be the wedding. I couldn't believe it.

That night, I decided to do some Googling about how to make *marudhaani* last longer. I just knew that it would be beautiful and I wanted it to keep for as long as possible. It said to exfoliate the skin, remove hair, and apply sugar water. Sugar water? That sounded sticky and gross.

I read further and saw that hair removal should be done at least a day prior if by shaving, and a few days prior if done by waxing. Looking down at my blonde hairy arms, I decided to take the risk and shave it. But it was two in the morning, and I would have to wait a few hours.

I had seen henna done at state fairs, but I had never gotten it myself and never seen proper *marudhaani* up someone's arms and over their feet. And soon, it would be me. I wondered how long it would take, how it would look, how it would feel.

But the worst part was that I wouldn't be able to use my phone the whole time because it would mess up the wet design.

That morning I shaved my arms for the first time, and it looked bizarre. The feel was even more strange. It was funny how the thin blonde hairs had been hardly noticeable before, but now that they were missing, it just didn't look right. I made sure to take a *head bath* just in case it was required.

The makeup woman came and began combing my hair. She was displeased and said something to Devi in Tamil.

"Did you not wash the hair? Saranya said it feels like greasy." Devi asked.

"Yeah, I washed it," I confirmed.

"But she said it is feeling too smooth. Did you use shampoo?"

"Shampoo and conditioner both, same as always."

"Don't want conditioner. It will make the hair flat. You want texture like this," she said as she pulled a strand of her frizzy hair from the towel she was using to dry her own hair.

I smiled politely and went to wash my hair again, without conditioner. It was going to be so difficult to comb in this humidity without conditioner. *It's just a few days of rituals*, I reminded myself. *Life will be back to normal soon, just adapt and take in the experience as a whole. They've adapted for you, you adapt for them. This is your chance to bond with his family, and you can't bond if you're being a diva.*

When I arrived back a half hour later with frizzy hair, there were more people in the bedroom that I did not recognize. I received many approving nods and, smiling shyly, wondered who they were.

"It is time for your facial," Devi announced.

But the thing is that my skin is extremely sensitive. If I even touch it, I'll have a pimple there the next day. I had to stop drinking milk because it gave me acne. The last thing I wanted was a new skincare regime just days before my wedding.

If this was any other time, it would be fine. But there was no way I would put myself at risk for zits in my wedding photos.

Since it had already been paid for, and she was already there, Devi happily laid on the bed to receive the treatment after my refusal. I smiled. She had been so kind and helpful through everything; she deserved a nice relaxing facial.

As she received the facial, my hair was tied into an elaborate style. I caught part of her Tamil, "*nalla mudi.*" She thought I had good hair, I smiled to myself. In a nation full of people known for having incredible hair, she thought that my hair was good. It was one of the best compliments anyone could ever hope to receive.

I had worn my normal daily makeup - a simple eyeliner, mascara, eyebrow tint, and lip balm.

They dressed me in a pink *saree*. It was stunning. The pink part was very light and almost transparent, and the border was a luminous shade of teal. The blouse wasn't made to match, but rather to be a sharp contrast in its dark shade of blue with the same border. I didn't want to ever take it off.

The final touches were then applied. Bangles, earrings, *pottu*, and jasmine. I was ready to begin my *marudhaani*.

I sat and watched the woman open a box with several cones in it and rub one in her hands, probably to make it warm so that it would spread more easily. But she didn't come to me.

She sat beside a woman on the floor. The facial woman took a cone and began working on a young girl. *Did I misunderstand something?* I tried to hide my confusion and continue looking around, smiling.

I couldn't do anything else. I couldn't really communicate with anyone. I could speak a miserable level of Tamil but could hardly understand anything. And they probably knew English but were as uncomfortable to speak it as my students had been. It would be rude to use my phone. So, I did what I was best at, staring at my feet. I imagined them soon adorned with brown paste and smiled. This was going to be so much fun, but I was so incredibly tired after not sleeping for days.

After the dozen girls in the room had finished, we went to the living room. Everyone sat on the floor watching me as I was directed to sit in a plastic chair in the middle of the room.

She pointed to my bangles and engagement ring, directing me to remove them. I sat them down on the little white TV dinner table and nervously gave her my hand. This was it.

She sat the *marudhaani* tip gently on the top of the inside of my forearm and drew a straight line horizontally across. Soon, the simple lines gave life to flowers, peacocks, chessboards, and mango paisleys.

I was surprised by how quickly she did it, and relieved that I had something to look at now instead of my feet. I watched her in silence, neither of us comfortable in the other's language, as everyone else chattered excitedly.

The photographer arrived and began to take photos of her applying my *marudhaani* and of the guests' *marudhaani*. Aarthi came beside me and started playing songs on a toy guitar to entertain everyone.

After both of the insides of my hands were complete, she spread sugar water on them just like the article said. Apparently, the stickiness helped to seal it and not crumble off as it dried.

While turning my hand to work on the back of my left hand, she accidentally smudged a piece and used her *dupatta* to remove the stain. She became more cautious, trying to avoid messing her work. It was almost hypnotic to watch the lines traced, and, before I knew it, I had finally fallen asleep.

I woke up to the bizarre feeling of a cold paste being applied to my feet. It tickled a bit but was largely soothing. I felt refreshed and calm for the first time in a week, and I relished in the tranquility.

"That is the specialty of *marudhaani*," Devi said from across the room. "It will make you relaxed before marriage."

I smiled back at her; it was definitely true. I'd been dreaming of sleep these past few days, but it eluded me at every turn. With the help of last night, just an hour of sleep had completely refreshed me.

Anooj walked through the door smiling. With all eyes on me, I smiled at him and quickly looked down to avoid seeming too eager. It wasn't too late for them to change their minds.

"How is it?" he whispered, nodding towards the work on my hands.

"Good, but I miss my phone."

He instantly cackled. "You should get *marudhaani* every day," he teased.

I tried to move my hand to see if it was still wet, but my arms were completely stiff, and it felt as though they were in casts. It started to feel itchy, and I began to panic, feeling a bit trapped.

"They will wash it off soon," he said softly as he inspected the designs.

The *marudhaani* artist began chatting with him in Tamil, and soon I was left again to my own devices. I watched her paint the lines on my feet as everyone else watched me.

Snacks began to be served, but I couldn't eat. Most of the guests' *marudhaani* was just on the tops of their hands, so they were free to do what they wanted, but Anooj had to feed me. I wished I could speak to him privately, but there was no chance. We couldn't really even talk on the phone.

With a stern look from his mother, he backed away apologetically. I was alone again.

One by one, the guests slowly began to leave, and I was left with my stiff hands and feet, unable to eat or walk or use the bathroom, or do anything else.

A young girl who seemed to be around eighth grade was watching me nervously from the corner of the room. I wondered why she hadn't left with the other guests as I quietly waved to say hi to her.

When a lot of people were in the house, I tried to avoid staring at anyone for too long, because I knew that we wouldn't be able to communicate, so I felt awkward. Maybe she would be more comfortable, though.

"You are Jurnee?" she asked meekly.

"I am," I smiled. "What is your name?"

"Kayal," she answered quietly. I took comfort in knowing that she seemed just as nervous as I was. "My father is the photographer," she nodded towards him.

"Great!" I said, waving to him as he waved at us.

"Do you want it removed? Are you hungry?" she nodded towards my stiff arms.

I wanted it to be dark, but I really wanted to pee. Devi noticed us chatting and pointed to the *marudhaani*.

"Still not removed, *aa*?"

I shrugged as she gave some sort of instruction to Kayal in Tamil. As Devi walked away, Kayal led me behind the house to a faucet.

"Tell me about America," she said as she began rubbing the crumbled bits of *marudhaani* off my hands.

"It's not quite as hot as this," I joked as I took in the sunset. "The sun sets past nine in the summer and before five in the winter."

"It changes?" she was shocked.

I tried to remember other big differences. "In the winter, ice forms on the road and makes it difficult to walk and drive."

Her mouth was agape as she began rubbing my other hand.

"No one pumps our petrol for us; we have to get out of the car and do it ourselves."

"Then how do you pay? It is he only that takes the money."

"We can go inside or there is a credit card payment built into the pump."

"What a strange place," she commented, and I smiled in agreement. They were indeed two vastly different places, both of which I absolutely loved.

"Would you rather grow up in America or India?"

I pondered for a moment, wondering what it would have been like to grow up in India. Anooj and my lives were almost polar opposites, but our fates had brought us together. What would it be like if we had the same background?

That night, I woke up again in the middle of the night. Why was the jetlag hitting me so hard on this trip and not on the others? I was going to look absolutely dreadful in the wedding pictures if I didn't get some rest soon. It was coming so soon, tomorrow we would be getting married.

Are you awake? I texted Anooj before seeing his WhatsApp banner "Last seen 12:06am." Great.

CHAPTER 12

Around noon, guests started arriving. I was instructed to greet everyone by saying "*Vaanga*" with my palms pressed together. They kept coming and coming, and soon, the whole living room was full.

I began to see familiar faces from Kerala entering. Radhika, Janaki, Devi, Sajith, and a few others. I was so relieved to see all of them.

Devu pressed her thumb and index fingers together and mouthed *super*. I wished that I could go over to them, but I settled for smiling and pointing back at her to say that she was super. She was wearing a pink puffy frock and looked exactly like a princess.

Snacks were served as I was ushered inside the bedroom by the lady who had done my hair the previous day. We smiled silently to one another as she began combing my hair. It felt a bit like a prom style, from what I could tell without seeing anything, and I was curious about what it would look like since there had been no demo. And I was curious as to why she was teasing my hair so much. It was going to be a rat's nest after this.

She's a professional, I said silently to calm my troubled mind. *She is going to do her best, and it will look great. Don't overthink. She wouldn't want you to look badly because it will ultimately reflect on her.*

I took a deep breath and tried to relax. This was way too much stress for my control freak mind.

When she finished, she handed me a mirror, and I looked closely. It looked very prom, complete with a bump. The back had a braid woven into a bun, and overall, I liked it. The bump was a little bit high, but there was nothing I could do about it now.

She then opened a small suitcase carrying dozens of makeup products. Were all of these going to be on my face? I looked around the room, concerned.

They all began laughing at my hesitation, and Devi came to my side. "Saranya will apply the makeup, don't be tensed."

But I was definitely tensed. My face was way too sensitive to use a stranger's makeup. Even a professional. Even with brushes and blenders instead of hand. I had spent years going through different brands before finding *one* that didn't give me pimples.

"Can you use my makeup?" I asked quietly, not wanting to offend her. This was going to be on my face for hours, and I really didn't want to have a hundred pimples on my wedding day.

She looked to Devi, annoyed, and they began speaking in Tamil. I could tell that I had just said something wrong.

I didn't mean to hurt anyone, so I tried to explain. "I have extremely sensitive skin and am worried about getting pimples."

"This is American brand makeup; you will not get pimples."

I tried to quiet my inner panic and compose my thoughts before speaking. "You can use anything you like, but I want to use my moisturizer and primer directly on the skin. Above the barrier, use what you like." That was an okay compromise, right?

Devi translated for her, and I looked at her nervously, hoping she wouldn't be upset. She shrugged, and Devi asked me to tell Aarthi where I kept my makeup.

She came back a few moments later with my small makeup bag, and I handed her my moisturizer and primer. She picked it up, read the labels, and nodded approvingly before beginning to apply them.

I'd never had my makeup done professionally before, and it was an odd sensation. I felt a bit like I was being painted with all the brushes, but I tried to lay back and relax.

When she handed me the mirror, I was shocked. I'd never worn lipstick or eyeshadow. My eyebrows were almost black. I looked like a completely different person.

She raised her chin, as though to ask me how it was. "Good," I replied, and she smiled. It was very evident that she was relieved, having surely pegged me for a diva based on our previous conversation.

"Jurnee!" a voice called from the door. Walking into the crowded room was Anooj's cousin's wife, Uma, from the *Poo Vaikkum* function.

"Hi! How are you!"

"Doing well, sorry we're late. You look great!"

"So you do!" She had a beautiful orange *saree*, perfectly pleated. They were done so sharply and neatly that she looked like one of the shop mannequins. I hoped to be at that level someday.

"Excited for your marriage?" she asked.

"Mostly nervous," I joked.

She smiled warmly, "Don't take tension. It will be over soon. Try to enjoy it as much as you can."

She was right.

Devi moved to the corner of the room and opened a box that contained a beautiful plaid *saree*. It was blue and pink, with a pink and gold *pallu* and a matching pink blouse. There was no defined border like most sarees have, but there were cute animals in the darker squares of the checkered plaid design, and the *pallu* had little tassels at the end.

It was gorgeous. And so soft, lightweight, and shiny. It was perfect. Anooj's family had impeccable taste in *sarees*. And I wished that I could buy a hundred more, all selected by them. I needed to learn how to wear them on my own first.

She handed me the petticoat and the blouse, and directed me to the bathroom to change. When I emerged, again very shy being in front of a dozen women that I barely knew, they were all very pleased with the blouse design. I didn't know Tamil well, but I certainly knew what pointing with nods and smiles meant.

A team stood, including Devi, Uma, and Saranya. Anooj's mother sat in the crowd, watching curiously but pleased.

They wrapped. They pleated. They pinned. And then they took a step back to admire their work. The crowd gave approving nods, and they began to open jewelry boxes.

A large piece of jewelry was pinned into my hair that fell over my forehead. Matching golden earrings hung in my ears with a matching golden necklace and belt. Pearls hung delicately from the gold details, and I was again impressed by the talent of his family in making these selections.

A large plastic box that contained dozens of bangles was opened. There were thin gold bangles, thick gold bangles, some blue ones that matched the *saree*, and they were all arranged symmetrically in a beautiful pattern. A small red *pottu* was pressed between my eyebrows, and a shiny silver *pottu* meant to resemble a diamond was pressed on my nose to look like I had a nose ring.

Devi inspected my face and smiled. The chatter among the crowd began growing louder. It was almost time.

A man walked through the front door and announced something in Tamil, causing the women to begin going outside. Before long, it was just the three of us remaining – Devi, Uma, and myself.

The photographer came back and began taking photos. I was never one who really enjoyed being photographed, so it felt very awkward, but I tried to stand nicely and follow his instructions. He took some of the three of us, then looked at his watch. "We're getting late," he beckoned.

"Get your bag and come," Devi said to me.

"What bag?"

"Your overnight bag."

"My overnight bag? Are we not coming back?"

"You will sleep there only."

What? Was that normal? Was that to prevent girls from running away the eve of their wedding? I'd much rather relax in the comfort of my own home than sleep at a strange place. *But maybe it will be like a nice hotel room,* I thought to myself. This could be okay.

I went to my suitcase and threw a few things in my backpack. Shampoo because I'd probably have to take a *head bath* since this was an auspicious occasion. No conditioner since it was apparently banned. Soap. Face wash. My own makeup to serve as a barrier. Comb. Contact case and solution. Phone charger even though I wouldn't be able to use it much. *That should do it,* I thought as I walked out of the spare bedroom.

"Did you get your fresh inners?" she asked.

I immediately went straight back into the room, forgetting to get fresh clothes for tomorrow. Apparently, there was a rule that every article of clothing had to be brand new and unused at your wedding, so I'd had to purchase new undergarments for the wedding. I grabbed a pair of pajamas also.

The three of us got into the car and made our way to the venue. I hadn't even seen it before. Most brides scout locations like they're buying a house. Going to each one, asking a thousand questions, finding out what's included, and then eventually settling on one. I didn't even know where ours was located.

It wasn't long before we reached our destination. It was much larger than I'd expected and had a parking lot laid with bricks. Our names were on a banner outside, and there were flowers everywhere. But more so, there were people everywhere, and I could feel myself start to panic.

Devi got out of the car first and instructed me to wait. I sat, noticeably shaking, as Uma held my hand. "Relax," she urged.

I tried to smile but was worried that I might vomit if I opened my mouth.

Devi stood outside my door, and Uma got out of the car. This was it. Devi opened my car door and took my hand in hers. Uma took my other hand, and the three of us walked through the gate. I wished my family had been here. Or my friends. Even the delivery guy from Domino's. I barely recognized anyone.

Someone waved to Uma, and she squeezed my hand with a smile as she went to them. *Please stay. Please stay. Please stay,* I silently urged Devi as someone came and draped a pink floral garland over me. It was beautiful, but much heavier than it had looked.

As we approached the stairs, I thought back to how I had almost fallen at Annual Day when I went up the stairs in a *saree.* I began to silently chant, *don't fall, don't fall, don't fall.*

Everyone was staring at me. Was it because I was a foreigner? Was it because I was the bride? Was it because they were curious about who was marrying Anooj? Probably a mixture of all three, just like before.

We finally got inside, and she led me onto the stage where I sat in a plastic chair. "Everything will be fine," she said with a smile as she walked away. "You are looking beautiful."

The back of the stage was decorated with a huge white cloth and bright yellow pillars. On the wall, our names and the date of the wedding hung painted on elaborate Styrofoam cut-outs. The lights were bright, my palms were sweaty, I was hungry but also felt sick at the same time. I didn't recognize any faces. Anooj was nowhere to be found. Tired of scanning the room for a familiar face, I looked down at my feet and traced the *marudhaani* patterns with my eyes. It was oddly soothing.

Finally, Anooj came, but he had an extra garland. Why did he get two? And why was he wearing a blue shirt with khakis? Why didn't he ever wear proper clothes? He smiled at me as he approached the stage, and two men came with a sofa.

"We'll sit there," Anooj whispered to me, softly instructing me to get up.

I got up and followed him to the sofa. It was red with gold details and beautiful designs extending past the sofa itself. It was gorgeous but extremely firm. Someone came and gave me a second garland to match his.

"Are you ready?" he asked.

"No," I replied. A little bit joking, but mostly serious. This was way more than what I had imagined. I tried to not look at him too much, to not give the wrong impression. So, I started tracing the *marudhaani* designs on my hands with my eyes.

"Look at the cameras, *da*."

I hadn't realized that they were taking pictures. I looked at him, slouching in the sofa like we were sitting watching TV. "Then sit up straight," I instructed him sternly. "Our grandchildren will see these photos."

He laughed and sat slightly straighter.

Suddenly, a man ran on stage and whispered something in his ear, and he sat up all the way.

"What happened? Who is that?"

"My school friend, Vasanthan," he replied. "Even he thinks I should sit straight."

"So, you listen to the police, but not to me?" I teased him.

"He is not police," he corrected.

"I know. I was joking."

He smiled, and I turned to look around the room. I wished that we could at least hold hands, but that would probably be scandalous. Instead, I looked around again for familiar faces. This time I saw a few and waved excitedly to them. Continuing to scan the room, I saw projectors showing live videos of our faces like a concert hall and realized that they were being broadcast from a drone that hovered in the center of the room.

Suddenly, a line began to form on the side of the stage. One by one, guests would come carrying a plate with two bowls built into it. One contained a yellow paste, and one contained a deep red powder. They smeared the paste onto our cheeks and hands, and pressed the powder onto our foreheads, sometimes onto the paste on our hands.

I wondered about the significance, but it was hardly the time to ask. I wondered why some did face and some did hands. I wondered if I was going to break out from this. Some brought leaves with money in them like at the *Poo Vaikkum* function. The reasons behind these actions must be really beautiful, and I was extremely curious about the meaning behind everything but I was unable to ask.

After the long line finished, we were directed to stand while we each were given a plate with clothes on them. Mine had the *lehenga*, but I wasn't sure what his was. It was gold and cream and looked nice. Would he finally wear proper traditional clothes?

We posed for a picture holding the new outfits, then went our separate ways to change. A team came with me to deconstruct the *saree* and to dress me in the *lehenga*. To my relief, the *lehenga* was much easier to wear, so it didn't take long, and they had even planned the colors to match well, so that I didn't have to change any jewelry. They were brilliant. Before we left the room, they wiped the yellow paste from my cheeks.

Devi took my hand again and led me to the stage. I was eternally thankful for her guidance, but too nervous to speak on it. I was enjoying the function, but there were literally hundreds of people, and they were all looking at me. It was overwhelming.

Anooj's outfit was a cream and gold jacket with gold pants and pointy golden shoes. There was even a matching scarf. He looked good, but I'd never seen this dress before in the movies I'd watched or with the people I'd met. I wondered why.

We stood in the center as some of the photographer's assistants came to carry the couch away, and we were each presented with a ring box.

"What is this?" I asked Anooj.

"The rings that we picked out."

"But we aren't married yet."

"These are the engagement rings."

"But we're already engaged." This was confusing.

"It's for show. Just exchange the rings when they say."

I kept awkwardly smiling, knowing that photos were being taken constantly. There was the lead photographer who gave directions, the secondary one who took close up photos of flowers, rings, *marudhaani*, outfits, etc. There was another who seemed to be taking video. One operating the drone. I was never certain where to look. I hoped they would be able to salvage my awful posing when they went to edit everything.

While facing the camera, we took turns sliding the rings on slowly while everyone watched and clapped. But just when I thought we were done, two of the assistants came carrying a table in front of us, and another carrying a cake.

The cake that we had ordered. I still found it odd that it was before the wedding, but at least it was here.

It was *enormous*. Three tiers, but not normal tiers. Each tier seemed tall enough to be three cakes. It was covered in white fondant with pink butterflies and said "Anooj <3 Jurnee." Chatter seemed to grow among the crowd, and people were pointing and gesturing at the cake.

"Is everything fine?" I asked Anooj.

"It is fine, they are just surprised that it is so big."

"Even I," I whispered, catching myself falling into Indian English again.

We each cut a piece and fed each other in slow motion for the photographers. But having it before the wedding struck me as backwards. The cake cutting *was* at the reception, but the reception was after the wedding. Why had it been before? Was this normal?

It was delicious and completely worth the five hundred rupee surcharge for being chocolate.

Just as quickly as the cake and table had arrived, they were taken away, and another line formed to the side.

"What is happening?" I whispered.

"They will click photos with us."

"All of them?" I asked, mouth agape. There were hundreds.

He chuckled at my dismay, "Just stand and smile, it won't take long."

One by one, each family came to greet us. Some gave gifts, some gave hugs. It was nice getting to finally meet everyone who came, but after about a dozen, I could no longer retain names or details. Everyone seemed so nice and affectionate. I had been worried that someone may say something snide about me being a foreigner, but no one seemed to mind.

By then, my students and their families had reached the front of the line. One by one, they came and congratulated me.

When it was Sajith's family's turn, his father turned to me and said, "Six months. I told you." The magic husband leaf had worked.

Three hours later, it was finished, and I was famished. The guests had all gone to eat after their photos so, naturally, I thought that it was our turn to go and eat.

It wasn't.

We were led outside by the photographer and his assistants for more photos. All I wanted was some cake.

He took many sets of photos and gave all direction to Anooj to convey to me how to stand and move. We took pictures hugging, twirling, walking. There were pictures with colored smoke, with rose petals, with water.

I was impressed by his concepts and overall vision for the photos and was happy to oblige.

We each had some solo pictures, then were released to have dinner.

Walking back into the venue and down the stairs, we came upon a room with several long tables like at Hogwarts. On each table was a long piece of paper. As soon as we sat, a boy who couldn't have been older than eighteen put a banana leaf in front of each of us and a team came, carrying metal buckets with big spoons.

Each one dropped a spoon of a different food onto our leaf, and before I knew it, there were eight different dishes with a big scoop of rice and a small cup of *payasam*. One man came to give a clear plastic container of a brown ball in a type of gravy.

"I had them get your favorite," Anooj whispered to me.

"It's *malai kofta*?" I asked, shocked.

He nodded and smiled, grabbing a second container for me. He was perfect. And tomorrow, we would be married. I felt my eyes begin to tear up with relief.

The photographer came back and took some pictures of us feeding each other as I coaxed the tears back inside. I wondered how many photos they had just of the reception and how many there would be tomorrow at the wedding. Was it normal to take so many photos? I didn't remember this many being taken at American weddings that I'd attended, but I smiled and followed their directions.

"I'll see you tomorrow?" Anooj asked rhetorically as he folded his banana leaf towards him to indicate that he was finished eating.

"You're going? What about the cake?"

"I think it's finished."

My heart sank. I had just a single bite of my own wedding cake. *Calm down, calm down,* I scolded myself. *You can have cake any time. This will happen only once. Relax.* "Oh," I mustered.

"Goodnight, Jurnee," he whispered with a smile, unable to show any affection.

"You're not sleeping here?"

"No, my house is nearby. I'll come in the morning."

I looked at my phone. It was nearly eleven, and the wedding was in just a few hours.

"You did really well, Jurnee. I know this is tough for you since it is unfamiliar and without your family, but you've done really well," he said softly as he stood to go.

I smiled, nervously. He was the only thing keeping me calm.

"I love you. I'll see you in the morning," he said as he put his hand gently on my shoulder, the maximum display of affection allowed.

Just then, Devi came with Aarthi, Kayal from the *marudhaani*, a young girl who held hands with Aarthi, and a woman.

"This is my friend, Geetha, she is the photographer's wife," she started. "She and her daughters and Aarthi will stay with you here. I will come in the morning."

She was leaving, too? I smiled hesitantly as she led the five of us to a room upstairs. There was a large bed, a large mirror, then two tables and a bathroom behind. Were we all going to share the bed? I looked around, wondering where we would all fit.

Geetha took a blanket and laid it on the floor, calling Kayal to sleep with her.

"No, no. You both please take the bed. It's okay."

"You are the bride," she said, very motherly. "Get proper rest."

"Are you sure? It's really no problem. I like to sleep on harder surfaces."

"Sleep in the bed, Jurnee *ma*. It is your wedding."

I nodded reluctantly and went to the bathroom to wash my face and change to pajamas. Aarthi and the other girl came to stay in the bed with me.

As I lie down on the bed and closed my eyes, I felt too nervous to sleep. *Tomorrow, you will be married,* I told myself. I wondered if it was normal to be absolutely terrified on the eve of your wedding. Not of marriage, but of being in the middle of a crowded function where you didn't know anyone or anything that was happening. As I drifted off to sleep, I wondered if it was too late to elope.

CHAPTER 13

I woke up to the sound of loud whispers. Devi had come and was talking to Geetha. The combination of hushed tones and Tamil meant that I couldn't understand a bit of it, but I was too tired to eavesdrop anyways.

My stomach turned, and I immediately felt sick. I was *terrified* of going in front of another crowd. I wondered if this one would be bigger or smaller than the previous night. *At least this is the last function*, I thought. *After this, you'll be married, and everything will be back to normal.*

I turned to look at my phone. It was only four in the morning. The wedding was in just a couple of hours, and I had only just gotten to sleep a couple of hours prior. How was I going to sit through this?

"Jurnee! You're awake!" Devi exclaimed as she hurried to my bedside in the dark. "Take head bath soon so we can get you ready. Saranya will be here soon."

I nodded sleepily as I got out of bed, grabbed my bag, and went into the bathroom.

"Don't want conditioner!" Devi shouted from the room.

I said a silent prayer for my hair.

Walking out of the room in a robe and with my hair wrapped in a towel, I had very mixed feelings.

I was marrying Anooj, the greatest person ever. My colleagues and students had come from Kerala. My in-laws were incredible and so welcoming. Every bride looks gorgeous, and soon, I would be one, too. But my family and friends weren't here. I didn't know most of the people. On the day that I was meant to be surrounded by longtime friends and family, I was surrounded mostly by strangers.

As much as my heart soared in seeing how much my in-laws cared for me and how everyone in Kerala supported me, it sank knowing that the people I'd known my entire life hadn't even tried to come. I was devastated but tried my hardest to hide it and carry on like everything was fine.

While Devi sat beside me to dry my hair, Saranya arrived and flipped on the lights, causing the three sleeping girls to groan and roll over simultaneously. Lucky them.

The three of them sat chatting in Tamil while she set up her makeup bag and silently gestured that I should give her my moisturizer and primer again.

I went to retrieve it and, when I got back, I was directed to sit in the chair. It was time. I leaned back as she instructed, closed my eyes, and tried to relax whilst being painted.

Chatter grew with time, and when I opened my eyes, there were about a dozen women in the room watching me get ready. I recognized a few, but most of them didn't seem familiar, and I didn't want to ask who they were in case I had already met them.

She turned me to look in the mirror, and I examined her work. My eyebrows were less harsh, the highlight captured my bone structure. I'd never worn red lipstick before, but it didn't look the way I had feared. I was pleasantly surprised.

Now that the makeup was done, she began combing my hair while chatting in Tamil with Devi. I fell back on my new favorite time pass of tracing my *marudhaani* with my eyes, which would have completely distracted me, had I not noticed her stitching something into my hair.

I tried to not show that I was alarmed, but I was definitely alarmed. What could possibly need to be *stitched* into my hair. Something snapped that sounded like a branch, and I smelled flowers. *Maybe it's just a lot of jasmine for everyone to share,* I thought to myself.

But it wasn't. I opened my eyes and saw the bump on my scalp like last night and several decorative items stitched into my hair. I couldn't get a clear view, but I wondered how they would come out afterwards.

She began braiding the black extensions into my brown hair, and for a moment, I wondered if Devi had been right about dying my hair, but dying your hair for a one-day event sounded a bit too drastic for me.

After the back of my hair was done, she began rolling the sides of my hair to give it more volume, and I looked like the brides in movies. She added a three-stranded golden piece that hung from my part and the sides of my hairline, meeting in the middle with a small golden *tikka* that hung onto my forehead.

Heavy earrings that had to be supported with golden strands that were pinned into my hair were added, plus tight golden cuffs that slid up as far on my arms that they would go.

"Keep the blouse and petticoat," Devi instructed me.

My stomach growled as I got up to put them on.

"Sorry, Jurnee. Here we do not eat before marriage. You will have marriage feast when it is over," she said reassuringly before adding very quietly, "But I will sneak *dosa* for you if you need to eat."

"It's okay," I replied. "I feel a bit sick anyway."

"Fever, *aa*?" she asked worriedly.

"No, just tension."

She smiled with a hint of concern as she went to retrieve the pre-wedding *saree*. I was to wear the *Poo Vaikkum saree*, then I would symbolically change into the marriage *saree*. It was very complicated.

I watched as they took it from the bag and opened it to reveal the blue and green *saree* that I hadn't seen in months. I couldn't wait to wear it again. I wondered if it was tradition to wear it for both events.

They draped it exceptionally fast, but I wasn't ready to go out in front of everyone again. I was absolutely petrified of not only going in front of a crowd where I knew precisely two percent of the attendees, but also where I didn't know what I was doing or what it meant. What if I did something wrong? Would the wedding be voided?

Devi led me again into the main room and up to the stage. On the way, we saw a rug with four men sitting on it. They were playing double-sided drums and one instrument that looked like the combination of a trumpet and a clarinet.

I smiled, not knowing where to look. Do I look to see my guests? Do I look at the cameras? Do I look at the ground to avoid panicking over how many people were here? I really wished my family had come. Just a shred of comfort from home would have made a world of difference, but I was alone. I tried not to dwell on it, but it kept coming to mind again and again.

There were about a dozen people on the stage between the men sitting with white *veshtis* and strings, close family that I recognized, and the photographer with his assistants. Why were they all on the stage?

I was instructed to sit on the floor just to the left of the center, from the audience's view. Sitting on the floor in a *saree* required some expert level maneuvering, and I carefully held the front pleats together so they wouldn't spread or become loose.

A man sat beside me, one of Anooj's uncles. *Where is Anooj?* I wondered but tried to remember that this was not an American wedding and I didn't know what's happening. Maybe it would be the groom who made the grand entrance.

Anooj's *chithi* and *chithappa* came to my side to drape a large white garland and a smaller red one. I recognized them and smiled, relieved that someone I knew was close by. We hadn't exactly *spoken*, but we had smiled at each other, and they were really sweet people.

Finally, Anooj came out. More khakis. Back to western clothes? Would he at least wear a *veshti* for the actual wedding part? I hoped so. He had looked so nice in it at Annual Day.

We exchanged a hidden smile, knowing that in a few hours we would be married. Or maybe sooner than that, I wasn't sure how long this was going to take.

The photographer and his assistants began milling about. Something was going to happen. I looked to Anooj, confused, to see if he possibly knew what was happening, but his response was to shrug.

His *chithi* and *chithappa* came to my side again with my wedding saree on a plate just like the night prior with the *lehenga*. Anooj also got fresh clothes from an auntie and uncle. Photos were taken from every possible direction before we were each led to our separate dressing rooms.

This time, we went back up to the bedroom rather than to the room downstairs where I had changed during the reception. Entering the room, each woman quickly took her station. One began unfolding the *saree*, one quickly identified the end to begin pleating the *pallu*, one began removing the saree I was already wearing, a couple were on standby waiting for directions, and *Saranya* was waiting to fix anything that came undone. It reminded me of the NASCAR breaks when they run around changing tires.

I went to the bathroom to change into the matching blouse. I was finally going to wear my wedding *saree*. The golden one with red flowers that this blouse was made to match.

It was beautiful but surprisingly thick. And as they opened it, I couldn't help but think that it seemed much longer than normal.

"Isn't this too long?" I asked her.

"This is marriage *saree*. It will be nine yards, not six."

I had totally forgotten, and the sudden realization that nine yards of thick fabric was going to be hanging on me with just safety pins terrified me. *Baby Jesus, don't let it fall down*, I silently prayed.

It took about twenty minutes for them to drape it to their satisfaction before my hair and makeup was inspected to be sure it hadn't been messed up. Everything was mostly fine, but they added a golden belt to the ensemble.

They all circled around me, inspecting every detail closely. I thought this meant that we would go back to the stage area now, but the photographer knocked on the door.

"Madam, ready?" he asked as the women stepped aside like the Red Sea.

I nodded, and he began to speak with Devi and Saranya in Tamil. I didn't catch a word but stood quietly waiting for direction.

He began pointing as his assistants started filling the room. One had a camera, one had a video camera, one carried lighting.

There were a variety of poses I stood in. Looking outside the window, both happy and sad, walking to the door, sitting in front of the mirror, pretending to have my makeup done again, pretending to have my hair done again, pretending to have someone straighten my *saree* pleats.

As someone who isn't even a big fan of selfies, it felt awkward, but he did a good job of getting me to relax, and I hoped that they would turn out well.

He took a couple of group pictures by request, then he and his assistants left as quickly as they had come.

Devi took my hand and looked at me with an endearing look more like a sister than a sister-in-law as she led me out of the room and down the stairs.

Everyone turned to look at me, but they didn't stand. "Here Comes the Bride" didn't play. My family wasn't there. My friends hadn't come.

But my new family who had accepted me wholeheartedly against all odds, my colleagues and students who I cared for so deeply, Anooj who was absolutely everything. I had all that I needed in this room, and, with a deep breath, we began down the stairs.

It took precisely three steps before I realized that I should have tightened the petticoat before they put the wedding *saree* on me. It was already loose, and the *saree* itself was so heavy.

Please don't fall down, I silently begged myself and the *saree*.

With each step, my gold bangles chimed, and my elaborate anklets made tinkling sounds. Making our way to the center of the venue and up to the stage, the stark contrast of arriving before the groom struck me. Surely, I had taken more time to be assembled than he had.

Before I could finish speculating, my favorite method for both overcoming and exacerbating my anxiety, Anooj began walking towards the stage.

He looked perfect in his long-sleeved white button-up shirt and white *veshti* with a gold stripe.

He took the seat beside me on the floor of the stage in front of several items.

There were banana leaves, a small fire, a coconut, some small bananas, several flowers, and a few metal plates. I looked at him, panicked. What were we going to do with all of this?

"Don't worry, they will tell us what to do. There is no exam," he whispered.

I smiled and nodded my head, catching myself in the famous side-to-side Indian nod. I had officially assimilated.

They began chanting and throwing various items into the fire. I turned silently to Anooj to make sure I wasn't supposed to do anything, but he nodded to confirm that we were just meant to be sitting.

They continued chanting, sometimes quickly and sometimes at normal pace. Did they have all of it memorized? One gestured to Anooj, and he started repeating their chants. A couple of times he pronounced something incorrectly, and they made him say it again. Was I going to have to do it, too? It would take us all day if I had to pronounce everything perfectly.

Suddenly, they were all looking at me. One of them whispered to Anooj who then whispered to me, "Pick up the coconut with rice three times."

I picked them up twice, but on the third time I was so nervous that I forgot to pick up the rice. *Did I jinx our marriage?* I wondered.

I looked at him, panicked, "I didn't pick up the rice. Should I do it again?"

He audibly laughed with a quick nod. I guess it was fine.

"Pick the coconut again," he instructed, translating for one of the priests. "Hold it while my *chithappa* ties the string."

I held it between my hands as he tied a yellow string that had a flower on it. I was so curious about the symbolism and turned to Anooj, "What does this mean?"

"No one knows the meanings. It is just tradition," he whispered back to me.

The only people I could potentially get answers from didn't understand me. I was doomed to never know, but smiled graciously to his *chithappa* as he finished tying the knot on my wrist.

Another uncle did the same to Anooj, and I watched in fascination. The chanting began to get louder. I looked at him, making sure that everything was okay.

"Everyone is going to come here in a second, don't panic," he assured me.

And sure enough, a small crowd suddenly gathered. Anooj lifted a yellow string with flowers hanging from it and maneuvered himself to tie it around my neck. I recognized this from the wedding scenes in movies. This was the equivalent of saying "I do."

As he tied it, Devi and his *chithi* arranged it to make sure it fell correctly. Everyone was throwing flowers. I saw Aarthi's excited smile from the corner of my eye. The photographer made Anooj hold the pose for a few minutes to make sure he got a good shot of everything.

And just like that, we were married. But it didn't seem to be over yet as Anooj took some turmeric paste on his finger and put it on the *thali* that would now hang around my neck forever. I remembered it being explained to me that it was only to be removed if one of us died or if I had a medical procedure. This thick gold necklace was a symbol of Anooj's soul, and I was to carry it with me always.

"Hold your fingers together like a cone," Anooj instructed me as we stood and he put his hand over my cone fingers. My *saree* felt loose. I wanted to sit back down. *Please stay up, please stay up, please stay up.*

A red cloth was wrapped over our hands, and we were led in a circle. His cousin held his hand, I held his hand, and Devi held my hand. The four of us walked in circles around the small fire.

"One more step," he whispered to me as they untied the cloth, and I was led to stand and place my right foot on a short pile of bricks.

As he was handed one of my toe rings, I realized that I had completely forgotten about them. He slid it over the second toe of one foot, and again for the other foot before giving a satisfactory nod to let me know that we were finished. I was supposed to also wear these until one of us died. I had so many articles representing my new marital status, why did he just have a ring?

The guests all watched intently, and the photographers milled around us taking photos from every possible angle. This was unlike any wedding I'd ever attended.

It was time for lunch, and then, since the reception was the day before, maybe I could take a nap.

But my dreams were quickly shattered when I found out that we would be taking more photos. I didn't mind them, and the photographer was really nice. Getting married was just so exhausting.

The photography drone came closer, and we took photos holding the garlands in heart shapes, him blowing rose petals at me, carrying me while rose petals fell around us, standing outside an onsite temple with a rainbow umbrella, silly poses with sunglasses, and traditional seated poses.

Some friends and students also came to take pictures with us, and I realized that the event I had been worrying about for months was over. I was relieved, but also wished I hadn't been so worried the whole time. It was hardly as stressful and difficult as I had thought that it would be. And now, it was just a memory accompanied by twelve thousand photos.

We went downstairs to eat, and it was as though a huge weight had been lifted from my shoulders. We were married, everyone was happy, everything was perfect. Until the photographer suddenly came.

Speaking quickly to Anooj, we were soon posing, holding food just outside each other's mouths as though we were feeding one another. I was so hungry, and now I sat pretending to eat. What cruel joke was this? But I played along; after each photo I was that much closer to finally getting to eat.

After he left, one of the catering boys spoke softly to Anooj as he passed by and, though my Tamil was rubbish, I caught a few words that sounded as though he was asking if my hair was real. Probably because the extensions made it extremely long. I tried to conceal my laughter so they wouldn't know I'd been eavesdropping.

One by one, my guests came to our table to say that they were leaving and to wish us a happy married life. Anooj's extended family began to filter out as well. I wondered how soon my nap would be, but it quickly became evident that it would probably not happen.

Anooj introduced me one by one to his friends - both school friends and college friends.

I recognized *the police* from the reception. "Is Anooj being a good tour guide?" Vasanthan asked.

I elaborated on the places I had visited – Sri Krishna Sweets, the *jigarthanda* place, Meenakshi Temple and my quest to see the inside, and, my personal favorite, seeing how spices were made.

"He took you to make spices? Seriously?" He turned to Anooj, "*Machi*, show her some nice places. She is a tourist here."

"I like the spice powder lady," I interjected.

He glared at Anooj, silently willing him to be the great tour guide that the Sri Krishna Sweets man thought he was.

Stepping away, Anooj introduced me to more family members. I knew five people at the whole venue and felt like a guest at my own wedding. I didn't even know if our families would ever meet, and my sadness flashed into anger for a moment. Not wanting to cry again, I pushed the thoughts away and turned to my newest comfort, tracing my *marudhaani* lines with my eyes.

After an hour or so of mingling, there was a sudden commotion.

"What's going on?" I turned and asked Anooj.

"We're going home," he said softly.

Maybe I would be able to take a nap now. I honestly wouldn't even mind sleeping with things stitched into my hair, I was absolutely exhausted.

The group was then divided in two. Half went home, and it seemed that the other half was to come with us. My nap was cancelled.

Anooj, his mother, and I climbed into the car and made our way to the house. When looking out the window, I noticed that the photographer was following us. What could he possibly want to take pictures of now?

When we arrived, they all got out, so I began to as well.

"Wait here," Anooj said as I watched everyone going inside. Why were there so many people?

After what seemed like ages, Devi came to bring me inside. I wanted to tell her how thankful I was for all her help with everything, but I didn't know how to convey the depths of my gratitude for all that she did. She had been instrumental in my ability to stay calm amid so much uncertainty, and I was forever in her debt. But more than that, our entire wedding had only happened because of her.

It was just past noon, and the three of us stood outside the gate. Anooj's close friends and family and the photographer waited inside. Devi told us to take off our shoes, and I looked at her hesitantly.

The bright Indian summer sun had been shining on the pavement, and my feet would certainly blister. I remembered back to the hostel days when they compared their feet with mine, and how much thicker the soles of their feet had been from running barefoot. There was no way that I could go barefoot on the hot cement.

She and Anooj insisted that I comply, so I did, and it felt as though I had stepped onto a stove. Was this how it felt to walk on coals? My eyes began to water involuntarily. It wasn't crying, but it alarmed everyone enough to throw water on our feet to cool us down.

It didn't work, so they told us to hurry inside, and the photographer's first images of me entering my in-laws' home looked as though I was crying.

We continued inside, and I was led to a chair in the living room so that I could be off my feet and relax. Devi went to tend to guests, and Anooj left to visit with his friends. I sat alone on my wedding day with burned feet.

After some time, Uma came and sat, but we were both tired and didn't really speak.

"Are you hungry?" she asked. "I can get something if you want to eat. Have you eaten today?"

"No, it's fine." I didn't feel much like eating. I was overwhelmed. I was tired. I was in pain. And the weight of everything in my hair was starting to give me a headache.

"Are you okay? Should we remove everything from your hair?"

I meekly nodded yes, and she immediately jumped to my side to begin pulling things out. She called Devi, and together, they began deconstructing.

First the heavy garlands were removed. Then they started on the jewelry. The heavy earrings, the *tikka* set that adorned my forehead, the arm cuffs, the belt. They removed the hair extensions and slowly worked their way up to the flowers.

I didn't understand a word they were saying, but I could tell that it was secured very tightly from the tension in their voices. What if it never came out?

Anooj's cousin's wife went to get some scissors and came back to release me. The pain was instantly gone, and I had never felt so relieved. What I hadn't realized, though, was that my hair had been teased a lot more than I thought it had been at the reception.

Devi went to get a comb and began gently trying to remove the tangles. *American weddings are so much less complicated,* I thought to myself as I silently thanked her for saving me.

I must have fallen asleep while she combed my hair because when I woke up, everyone was gone. I went to the bathroom to wash up and noticed how dreadful I looked. The makeup was far past its prime, and I washed it off with water, unsure whether my things were here or at Devi's house.

When I got back to the living room, Anooj was waiting for me.

"Finally woke up, *aa*?" he asked.

I rolled my eyes, "Indian weddings are exhausting, okay?"

"I know. You did really well, though. I know it was overwhelming for you, and with so many people, and without your family. I've said it before, but you have nothing to worry about. Everyone likes you."

I started to cry.

"What happened? Go and change if you're uncomfortable. Your bags are just there, no need to keep wearing a heavy *saree* at home."

"No, I'm just so tired, and I was so afraid of everyone not liking me."

"Why would you be afraid of people not liking you? You're perfect."

"Ha," I said, rolling my eyes. "I know how people feel about marrying outside of language and religion and caste and everything. And I'm so opposite of who they were imagining for you."

"Nonsense. They were imagining someone who has a good heart, and that is who I married."

I smiled and took a *churidar* from my suitcase.

"You can just wear pajamas if you want, no one is coming."

"What do you mean?"

"They will come only tomorrow after breakfast."

"Why? Is everything okay?" Had I upset someone or had something happened?

"Everything is fine. It's *first night*."

I looked around and realized there were flower petals strewn around the room. "The first night of what?"

CHAPTER 14

I woke up in an empty house and looked around the room. A TV hung on the wall beside the window, whose sill held a router and a bowl of bangles. A closet was built into the wall and cleverly disguised to look like a small cupboard and not take up a lot of space. A couple of chairs lined the wall, and the sun shone brightly through the curtains.

Where was Anooj?

Looking at my phone, I saw it was just past eight. I stayed in bed, scrolling through Facebook, when I saw *my husband* come through the door with bags of food.

"When did you wake up?" he asked.

"Just now," I replied with a yawn.

"I brought *vada* and donuts and *dosa,* and I found Cheerios and milk at the store if you want any."

"Why so much food?"

"It's our first full day married, and I wanted you to have all of your favorites."

I jumped from the bed and hugged him. How did I get so lucky?

We sat on the floor and had an absolute feast. After two days of functions, I just wanted to stay in this room and sleep for a week.

"Don't forget, we have the feast today afternoon," he reminded me. I had completely forgotten about the feast. It was to be only meat, and my anxiety wheels were turning a mile a minute.

"What will I do, though? I'm vegetarian." I didn't want to give the diva-foreigner impression to anyone, but I certainly couldn't eat anything there.

"We'll manage. Don't get tensed," he said as he passed me another *vada*.

"When do we go?"

"We'll go to my sister's house after a few hours."

"Who all is going?"

"Everyone."

"Is this the last function?" I asked, hopeful.

"Yes," he said with a laugh. "Then you can relax. And our honeymoon is soon also. I know it's tough for you as an introvert to be in the center of things, but I promise it's almost over. And this is the only visit you will have that will be like this, after this it will be normal relaxed visits only."

That was a relief. I genuinely liked everyone, just not being in front of them.

Anooj turned on the TV, and we watched a singing competition as we devoured our multicultural breakfast.

Before we knew it, a few hours had passed, and we had to get ready to go. I couldn't drape a *saree* by myself, so I took a quick shower and settled for a *churidar,* even though I struggled to pin the *dupatta* to my shoulders symmetrically.

I combed my hair and braided it, adjusted the yellow string necklace that he had tied onto my neck, admired my slowly fading *marudhaani*, put in a pair of gold earrings and gold bangles, and went to meet Anooj.

"How is it?" I asked him, hoping for approval in my first Indian outfit that I chose without help.

"Perfect, but missing a few things."

My heart sank.

"No *pottu* or *kumkum*?" he asked.

I had totally forgotten and immediately went to grab a *pottu* from my bag. "I don't have *kumkum* though," I said, mildly panicking.

He laughed. "My mother does. Don't worry for everything."

He was right, and I followed him to another cupboard that had little god statues in it. Watching as he opened a tiny silver dish, I saw a pile of fine red powder and tilted my head towards Anooj as he placed a pinch of it on the edge of my hairline above the *pottu*.

"Perfect," he said as he closed the bowl and the cupboard. "Ready?"

"Ready," I smiled nervously.

We walked out of the house, locking the door and gate behind us, and made our way to his motorcycle. He got on to turn it in the correct direction and start it before motioning me to climbed onto my now familiar side saddle position.

Everyone looked at us, and I looked down. My toe rings were loose, and I was careful to angle my feet upwards so that they wouldn't fall off. *Would I have to do this my whole life? Was there a way to make them tighter, or was it too late to get a pair that fit better?* I wondered.

I looked up for a moment but saw that everyone was still staring, so I decided to continue looking at the ground until we reached the feast. I had never realized how uncomfortable it was to be stared at until I arrived in India for the first time. They were soul piercing and made me extremely uncomfortable.

Finally, we arrived and walked into Devi's house, met with excited greetings and a more excited Aarthi, who immediately took my hand and led me to her toy collection. I wished that she knew how much I valued her presence, but I had no idea how to phrase it in a comprehensible way.

It wasn't long until we were brought back into the living room to be among everyone. They all chattered merrily in Tamil, and I traced my fading *marudhaani* lines with my eyes for a distraction.

Anooj noticed my boredom and filled me in in a whisper. "They're finalizing the food donation for the reception, marriage, and non-veg feast," he said.

"What food donation?"

"It is normal here that, in marriages and functions, we order a lot more than what we need so that the caterer can give it to an orphanage."

It was the sweetest thing I'd ever heard. "Can we go?"

"Go where?"

"To serve the food for them."

"You mean us? You and me?"

"Of course. It is from our wedding, we should serve them."

"There isn't time."

"It's just an hour or two," I insisted.

"Next time," he promised.

I looked down, defeated.

"I mean it, Jurnee. Next time we will, even if we have to organize a function for no reason. We really won't have enough time."

I half smiled at him, hoping he meant it, as everyone started to stand and go to the terrace for lunch.

Out of the corner of my eye, I saw Janaki and Radhika reaching the house and waved excitedly for them to join us.

"How are you!" I exclaimed as they wrapped me in hugs.

"You were so beautiful in the wedding!"

"We're so happy for you!"

We reached upstairs and walked to the table to eat. They hadn't been exaggerating. Despite there being numerous dishes, not one was vegetarian.

Anooj came to sit beside me. "All okay?" he said with a grin.

"No. What am I supposed to eat?" *Don't be a diva-foreigner, Jurnee. Don't be a diva-foreigner.*

"You can eat the gravy. There isn't meat in it."

He wasn't serious, was he? My face dropped.

"I'm joking only. We have some special dishes for you. Relax."

I was half angry, half relieved. At least he hadn't been serious.

We sat at the long tables, Hogwarts style again, and one by one, the guests left after they ate. My students and colleagues as well.

They each ran to bid me farewell, all of us sad that we didn't know when we would next meet.

"Come back to hostel soon, Jurnee Miss," Devu pleaded.

"I will try," I said as I tucked her hair behind her ear.

"We'll email you!" Radhika and Janaki promised.

I did my best not to cry as I hugged them one last time and waved goodbye to their parents.

As all of the other guests eventually made their way to their respective homes, we went downstairs to sit for some time. With no other guests or distractions, I prodded Anooj and nodded to my toe rings, reminding him how loose they were.

He nodded his head and began to speak to his mother and sister in Tamil.

There was laughter, then a tone like *how do you not know this* as Devi turned my foot on the side and showed us that the toe ring had a seam. Apparently it was adjustable, you just needed to press it. Anooj and I looked at each other, both feeling very stupid.

"Do you want the permanent style instead?" she asked me.

There was a permanent one? "Sure!" At least then we wouldn't have to deal with flimsy metal being stretched and worn.

"I'll just call the jeweler," she said as she opened her phone.

I was getting new toe rings.

The next morning, Devi and her family came to the house for breakfast. I had been instructed by Anooj and his mother to be dressed nicely because guests were coming, but I hardly considered them to be guests. Why had I dressed in one of my *churidars* with gold jewelry? Maybe the jeweler was coming, and they wanted me to look decent.

We sat outside in the backyard beneath the guava trees and coconut trees, when suddenly a man came.

"He is our neighbor," Anooj whispered to me.

He greeted the family, then turned to me asking, "*Nalla irukkeengala?*" to ask how I was, though literally it meant *are you good*.

I had heard *eppadi irukkeenga* asking how you are, but not phrased *nalla irukkeengala*. I was torn on using the standard answer of *nalla irukkaen* to say that I was good, or a simple *aamaa* to confirm.

Everyone was looking at me, so I gave the short *aamaa*, and everyone laughed. It was the wrong answer.

The neighbor looked extremely puzzled as Anooj explained to him in Tamil, probably to say that I had taken his question literally because then he began to laugh also.

After a few minutes more of chatting in Tamil with everyone, the jeweler came, so he bid his farewells.

I was surprised how thick the new toe rings were as I turned them in my hand, looking down at the ones on my toes for comparison. These were very classic, simple, cylindrical, and thick. Mine were cute, but thin and flat. I really liked the permanent ones.

The jeweler looked at my toes, toe rings, and his collection before deciding on a pair to use. He turned to me, "You want it to be tight, but if this is too tight, then say."

How did I know what was too tight? I'd never worn anything on my toes before a couple of days ago. I nodded in confirmation, and he sat the chosen set aside as he gave Anooj directions in Tamil that apparently told him to go bring a bucket of water and a bar of soap.

Anooj sat at my feet, and everyone else sat on my sides to watch. He immersed my foot then rubbed the soap on it and slid the toe ring down. I felt it slide over the knuckle of my toe and winced in pain. Was that normal or was that the *too tight* that he had mentioned? The toe ring was at the base of my toe, like a ring on your finger.

He began scolding Anooj in Tamil, gesturing towards my toe. He pointed at where it was, and then pointed again just above that knuckle. Apparently Anooj had slid it on much too far.

"Are you okay?" Anooj asked, worried. "I have to slide it back over the knuckle now. I'm sorry," he added with a worried grimace.

I shuddered as he pulled it back over the knuckle, but it wasn't as bad as I had anticipated. At least it was over. A second one slid above it in a pair, before he switched and did the same for the other foot. All four were done.

Everyone gathered around to inspect them, and I heard *nalla* several times. I really liked how they looked, and I was glad that everyone else did, too.

He stayed for some time, and everyone sat around chatting. I listened to them speak in Tamil, but instead of tracing the *marudhaani* lines with my eyes, I stared at my new toe rings.

Something was odd, though, my toe was slightly blue. I touched it and realized it was numb. Had the toe ring been too tight? Had I lost circulation? What if my toe needed to be amputated? *Whoa there, Jurnee,* the normal part of my brain chimed in. *You don't need an amputation, just try to get it off.*

I tried to pull off the ring, it wouldn't budge. I tried to twist it, but it wouldn't budge. It was stuck, and my panic began to grow. I gently elbowed Anooj to get his attention, and he lifted his eyebrow to silently ask what happened.

I nodded down at my toe, "It's blue and numb," I whispered.

He immediately interrupted everyone and said something in Tamil that caused quite a stir as they all gathered around me.

"Is it paining?" Aarthi asked me, concerned as she held my hand worriedly.

Anooj came quickly with the water and soap again to try to get it off. He tried to pull the rings toward him, but they wouldn't move. Devi tried. Naren tried. The jeweler tried.

They looked at each other, puzzled, until Anooj's mother said something in Tamil.

Anooj came now with a small canister that seemed to contain oil. He smothered my toe in it and tried to pull the rings toward him, but they still wouldn't move.

I couldn't understand them, but I could hear the worry in their voices. This was bad.

Anooj took the bucket and came back with it again. I looked at him, furrowed brow, and he shrugged saying, "Hot water."

Dipping my toes into it, it was more than hot. It was *scalding*. Shouldn't it be cold to constrict the blood vessels?

"Keep your foot there for some time," Devi instructed me, and I flinched as I submerged my entire foot. Maybe I should have just kept the adjustable toe rings. What had I done?

After a couple of minutes, they all tried again. Not even a millimeter of movement. It was starting to hurt now. I could feel my heart beating through my feet.

"What about string?" I asked, throwing out any solution that I could think of.

"What do you mean?" he asked.

"If you wrap it around the toe, it will constrict it, and might allow the toe to be thin enough for the ring to pass over again," I replied as I pulled up a video on YouTube to show him.

"Genius!" he exclaimed, as he showed the video to the others and explained what the next steps were. Anooj got up again and came back with some string. Hopefully, this would work.

It hurt a lot. My toe was wrapped without even a sliver of skin showing, and it was an intense pain that I hadn't felt before. I had never realized that my toes were this sensitive.

After they finished wrapping it to the edge of my toe, it was time for the true test. Would it come off?

They each took turns again, trying to pull it off. And one by one, each failed.

What would happen if it never came off? Would my toe just shrivel up? Would I still be able to walk properly? I'd read about people having difficulty walking without their big toes for stability, was there any issue with the second toe?

They started murmuring in Tamil, and soon, the jeweler got up and left.

"What happened?" I asked Anooj.

"He is going to get some pliers."

"Sorry. Pliers?" Like, the tool?

"Yeah. There's a small seam in the ring, and we're going to pull the ends apart from each other to hopefully get them off."

That sounded painful, but I nodded in agreement. This was our last resort, nothing else could probably be done without cutting off my toe. *Please, baby Jesus*, I silently pleaded.

Everyone looked at me worriedly. Aarthi held my hand again. I was terrified but tried not to show it. I was genuinely surprised that, until now, I hadn't cried even a little. I hadn't even cursed.

The jeweler came back with a small yellow cloth shopping bag full of tools, and I felt my mouth go dry. It was like the beginning of a torture scene in a spy movie.

"Ready?" he said confidently.

I smiled weakly to indicate that I was, but I was unable to form words. I was terrified.

"It'll be fine," Anooj tried to comfort me, but it was useless.

The jeweler took one set, and Naren took the other. Anooj stood above them to give direction. The three of them looked to me for confirmation to begin, and I reluctantly nodded as I closed my eyes.

The pain was intense. It felt as though they were pulling my toe off and not the ring. I squeezed the side of the sofa and prayed that I wouldn't cry or shout or curse. My eyes were squeezed shut so tightly that even they began to hurt.

Suddenly, a figure came beside me and cradled me. I wasn't sure who it was, or what the protocol was for this situation. She placed my arms around her and patted my head. It was Anooj's mother.

The first ring opened, and it hurt more for a brief moment, but then went back to being numb. There was still another ring on the toe. They had to start again, but there was a brief celebration of getting it off my toe without my toe falling off. I owed them my life. Or, at the very least, my toe.

The second one went more quickly since they knew what to expect. With both rings off the toe, the pain was sharp and sudden. Someone began pressing the toe to encourage blood flow to resume as they began on the third ring. And then the fourth.

Once completely free, I squeezed another hug to Anooj's mom to silently thank her for being there and thanked everyone for their work.

"So adjustable is fine, right?" Anooj joked as he put the old toe rings on the table.

I saw the misshapen remains of the four permanent toe rings and agreed. I liked the style of the permanent ones more, but I didn't want to risk my toes falling off again.

"Wake up," Anooj prodded me the next morning.

Groggily I wiped my eyes and stretched. "What?"

"We're going to our family temple today."

"Your family built a temple?"

"No. It's our ancestral temple."

I didn't even know my great-grandparents' names or anything about them, and he knew the exact temple that his had visited.

His mother and sister dressed me in a soft pink cotton *saree*, complete with bangles, earrings, *pottu*, *kumkum*, and jasmine, and by the time we finished, Anooj had come back with the rental car.

It was a three-row SUV with Anooj and Naren in the front, myself and Devi in the middle, and his mother and Aarthi in the back.

We stopped at a roadside restaurant for breakfast. Their house was just behind it, and their children played outside. There was a plexiglass box in the very front where a man stood making *parottas*, and I instantly grew hungry.

"What do you want?" Devi asked.

"*Dosa* is fine," I replied.

"Only *dosa*?" she joked. "No chutney or *sambhar*?"

I smiled, "Tomato chutney."

We all sat as they brought out the food and, one by one, the man holding the suspended tray with four deep vessels that resembled vases gave us our choice between the chutneys and *sambar* that he would scoop for us onto our banana leaves.

"Thank you," I said as he gave me my chutney, internally scolding myself for forgetting to say *nandri* instead. Force of habit.

About an hour later, we arrived at the temple. It was large and made entirely of thick blocks. There were a few pillars in the room, but it was largely empty apart from the dozens of people who sat inside.

I wondered what they were doing. At church, we go when there is a sermon, not just to sit. But here, people were coming and sitting peacefully with their families, children were playing in the corner, and there was a chicken on the loose.

Anooj's mother led us to a back room where men with white *veshtis* and strings were standing. They said something to Anooj, and he positioned himself laying on his stomach, facing them. Was I going to have to do that, too? In a *saree*?

The turned to me, and I panicked. There was no way, and I looked at Anooj and his mother with concern.

"You only need to kneel with your forehead to the floor," he said.

That wasn't so bad. I did as instructed, then we were both given *tulsi* water and a tray of fire to take blessings from. We took turns holding our hands above the fire to absorb the heat, then bringing our palms over our head.

The first few times, I was very nervous about the fire, but it subsided a little bit each time we had to do it.

We went behind a curtain, and there were more of the men in white *veshtis* and strings there. They chanted for about ten minutes, then we were released to go back and sit with Devi and her family.

"What just happened?" I asked.

"Now our wedding is official."

"It wasn't already?"

"Not until we take blessings in our ancestral temple."

Things were much different here than they were back at home.

When we got back to the house, we began preparing lunch. Anooj's mother and sister and I pulled peas from pods. They didn't come in a can here. They bought a bag full of pea pods, and we spent almost an hour getting them all out.

A few times I tried to put the brownish ones in the bad pile, but she wouldn't put them there unless they were black and slimey. Even if the pod itself was blackened, she would still open it to see if any peas were salvageable. They wouldn't waste even a single pea. I felt awful for all of the vegetables I'd wasted in my life.

While Anooj's mother took the peas that were ready to be cooked, Devi took another bag full of small white jasmine flowers and began making chains. I always thought that they bought the jasmine chains from the man down the road, had they been making them all this time?

I sat and helped her sort the flowers so they faced the same direction, and it would be easier for her to tie them to the string. It was a tedious process, but I sat in silent awe of how much care she took for each one. How much time they must spend for this daily to remove peas from pods and to tie tiny flower stems onto a string. I immediately felt like a lazy slug.

After we finished, Devi began sweeping the floor to pick up dirt and other debris from the pea pods and flowers, and I didn't want to be useless so I went to the kitchen and started washing the dishes.

Anooj's mother glanced over and didn't say anything, but her smile said enough. Against all the odds, I was not only accepted in the house, but I was welcomed and appreciated. I wished that we could stay.

But we couldn't. We were set to leave for our honeymoon to Ooty that night, and then I'd be back to the US shortly after. I wasn't ready to go home just yet. I *was* home. Home is where your heart is, right?

CHAPTER 15

We got our backpacks, had a quick *dosa* dinner with his mother, and said our goodbyes. We were finally going on our honeymoon, and I couldn't stop beaming.

I hadn't taken a bus in India before and was curious if it would be similar to the train experience that I had in Kerala.

"Excited?" he asked.

I rolled my eyes with a chuckle. Wasn't it obvious? "How far to Ooty?"

"Just a few hours, but we have a bus transfer in Coimbatore, so it will be a little longer."

The pictures I'd seen of tea growing on rolling hills were spectacular, and to think that he lived just a few hours away from it. We had discussed a few other places to go, namely Rajasthan and Sikkim, but they weren't possible as Rajasthan is extremely hot in May, and Sikkim has a lot of travel limitations for foreigners.

The bus stand was much more crowded than I had anticipated. There were easily at least two hundred people, even late at night. There were buses everywhere, and none of their labels were in English, so I just followed Anooj like a baby duck.

I instantly scolded myself for complaining about the boards not being in English. *They have been living here for centuries, and you have been here for five minutes, why would the boards be in English? Obviously, they will accommodate local people. When you travel, you adjust for locals. They don't adjust for you.*

After my trip to Kerala, I had found myself being a lot more patient back home. I took extra time to understand people who struggled with English, and I took extra time to give clear directions to people who were passing through. Having been in those situations made me realize how scary it can be in a new place, and how imperative it is that we take care of each other.

After two rounds around the giant parking lot, we found the correct bus and got on.

I had been expecting a fusion between American charter bus and city bus, but it was the most luxurious bus that I had ever seen. There were beds with silky curtains, TVs, outlets - both USB and standard, complementary bottled water and snack bag, pillows and blankets.

"How much did this cost?" I gawked. I didn't want to waste the whole budget on the bus ride.

He paused, "Probably thirty dollars."

"Each?" It would have easily been five times that price back home.

"Thirty total." He noticed my mouth agape. "We are not as greedy about money here," he teased.

I sat my bag in the corner behind my head and stretched out. Fifteen dollars for this luxury, it was unbelievable. But when I awoke to loud, scary shouting, the facade of luxury quickly fell off.

"Why are they shouting so much?" I asked as I rubbed my eyes.

"Because it's time to get down."

"They don't need to shout for that, though. I thought we were being attacked."

"That is how buses are," he shrugged.

And with that, my adoration for the fancy bus had melted away.

We took our bags and went down to a much smaller bus stop. It seemed to be a travel agent's office, and we sat in plastic chairs with about a dozen other people. Were they all coming with us to Ooty?

After about a half hour, I suddenly had to pee. Looking around, this hardly seemed like a place that would have an American toilet, so I tried to ignore it.

Ten minutes later, it was back and even worse than before. Anooj saw my leg shaking, a failed attempt at distracting myself, and asked what happened.

"I have to pee," I whispered.

"There's a toilet back there," he pointed the side of the building, an unlit area with a few trees and a group of men standing drinking tea nearby.

Yes. I was going to go walk in the dark past strangers in the middle of the night wearing a ton of gold. Great idea.

"Do you want me to come with you?" he asked, sensing my panic.

He was perfect. And I was a child needing an escort to the bathroom. Bless him for dealing with me.

He carried both of our bags as we walked into the dark, past the men drinking tea, and he stood outside the door to wait.

To my surprise, it was an American toilet. But not to my surprise, there was no toilet paper and no soap. I reminded myself to be thankful for the little wins and stepped out to join him.

The next bus was just as fancy, but also came with just as much shouting. But there would be no more buses for a few days. We were in Ooty.

The air was cool, like an Illinois spring, at least a twenty degree decrease from Madurai. I almost wished that I had a jacket. In India. In May. It was unbelievable.

We each carried our backpacks up a small hill that led the way to a line of yellow *autos* patiently waiting. He stood beside the first one and gave the name of our AirBNB to the driver. When the driver nodded to accept our fare, we got in the back - me first into the side with the protective edge, and Anooj on the side with the opening.

After just a couple of minutes, we arrived, and the *auto* driver gave Anooj his cell phone number so that we could call him later.

We got out and walked towards a blue and white cottage surrounded by greenery. It looked like a storybook, and I'd never seen anything like it in real life. We walked inside and met with the owner, a young British woman and her large guest record book that reminded me of the hostel book that logged the times we came and went.

She took copies of our IDs and then showed us to our room.

The floors were hard wood with a bit of creaking. The bed had four posts like in old movies. The air was a little cold, but there were heavy blankets and even heating pads available. A huge fireplace sat just opposite the bed, and it was the perfect honeymoon spot. But first, I just wanted to sleep.

We woke up that evening and checked online to see if there were any events going on. It turned out that there was a flower festival nearby, so we got ready.

As we walked out the door, I yawned.

"Still tired?" he teased me.

"These past couple of weeks have been hectic. I just need to rest. Everything is done, right? No more functions ever except as guests?"

"Until we have kids. Then it all starts again.

I looked at him in horror, and he laughed while pulling me closer in a hug. "I'll always be beside you. Don't worry so much."

We stood for a moment before entering the foyer again. The British woman stopped us on our way out. "Would you like Indian or continental food for breakfast?"

We looked at each other to silently ask the other their preference, and Anooj replied, "We'll have one of each," so that we could try a bit of everything.

The sun was beginning to set, and it had gotten almost *cold*.

Trying to keep me warm but still abide by India's unwritten public display of affection laws, he turned to me and asked, "Should we buy a jacket?"

We were actually going to buy a jacket in India in May. I couldn't help but to laugh.

The streets were very crowded, but not with cars. There were people milling about everywhere, and we finally found a small shop that seemed to sell sweaters.

The woman at the register greeted us saying, "*Vanakkam*," with folded hands while the man in the back nodded. "Do you need help to find anything?" she asked.

"We're looking for a sweater for her," Anooj told her.

"Ah, yes. It is cold here, but you are a foreigner, no?" she turned to me. "Isn't it hot for you?"

I smiled politely, unsure of how to respond.

She led us to the racks of women's sweaters, and I looked through them. They had a good variety of different colors, fabrics, weights... but nothing really stood out to me.

Scanning the room, I saw the perfect navy-blue hoodie that I needed and nudged Anooj to tell him to follow me.

"Dear, that is the men's section."

Putting it on over my *churidar*, it fit perfectly. A little bit too big, a little bit too long of sleeves, huge pockets. I turned to Anooj, beaming.

"Do you like it?" he asked rhetorically as he followed me to the counter. I didn't even want to take it off, it was so soft. She charged us more than what I would pay for it back home. Foreigner tax struck again.

Walking back out into the street, I asked Anooj, "Why didn't you try to haggle?"

"I don't like to."

"But I thought it was required to shop in India that you be able to haggle."

"And that is why I don't like to shop," he said with a small chuckle as he held my hand. We hadn't held hands in public before. I moved closer and leaned my head on his shoulder. "Are you hungry?" he asked as we passed a restaurant whose sign said they had pasta. "If you are tired of Indian food, we can go here."

I loved Indian food, having lived previously in a village in Kerala for months, but I did miss western food. It had been weeks, and the thought of pasta made my stomach growl.

We were the only ones in the restaurant, and their menu was bigger than The Cheesecake Factory menu. They had pasta, pizza, tacos. But how authentic would it be? That was the true question.

"Do you want to share or get different meals?" Anooj asked.

"We'll share from different?" I was starving, and luckily, the waiter came quickly.

"Madam, Sir. What will you have?"

Anooj nodded at me to begin. "I'll have the fettuccine alfredo."

"And I'll have the chicken tacos," he finished.

"Anything to drink?"

"One bottle of water," Anooj replied.

"Cold or room temperature?"

"Room temperature," I interjected. I was already freezing; there was no chance was I drinking cold water.

He nodded and took our menus, leaving Anooj and I alone. His brown eyes twinkled in the dim room, and his hair was starting to grow out from the wedding haircut. "What is it?" he asked.

"Why don't you speak to anyone in Tamil? Aren't we still in Tamil Nadu?"

"A lot of the people who work here aren't Tamil. They have shifted here to work at a tourist place and earn for their families."

"Do their families come with them?"

"Sometimes, but they can't always."

My heart sank.

"They go home sometimes, don't worry. Even in America, people will travel to New York or LA for a job, no?"

He was right, but somehow it seemed worse with a language barrier. Tamil was so difficult to learn; I knew firsthand.

"So, what do you want to do tomorrow?" he asked, changing the subject.

"We'll go to the flower festival?"

"Okay, sure. And don't forget, the photographer will come the day after."

I had almost forgotten that our photography package included the photographer coming on our honeymoon for a day to take some photos. It seemed like such a strange concept, but the pictures would be gorgeous with all this scenery.

"And I have one surprise for you after dinner."

"What is it?"

"You have to wait for after dinner," he said seriously, to which I looked at him sadly. I wanted to know now. "Okay, fine," he sighed, "Ooty is famous for one thing."

"For tea?"

"More than tea."

"Hills?"

"More than hills."

"I don't know. Just tell me."

"After dinner."

I sighed, but luckily the waiter came back with our dinner. He sat the chicken tacos in front of me and my fettuccine alfredo in front of Anooj. "Will there be anything else?"

"Actually, sorry, I'm vegetarian."

He gave a slight gasp, then apologized, "I'm sorry, madam. I thought he will be the vegetarian."

"It's okay," I said with a smile, realizing that stereotypically it would be the Indian who was vegetarian and the American who was not. He quietly switched the plates and walked away.

I had had my doubts about the pasta, but it was surprisingly delicious. It had been so long since I had had cheese, I wanted to cry. "How is it?" I asked him.

"It's okay. I always wanted to try a taco, but it isn't great."

"We'll get some in the US," I promised.

"Speaking of the US," he started. "Have you thought about where you want to live?"

"I'm not sure," I admitted. I loved my home, but Anooj's family was so sweet, and India was absolutely enchanting. I didn't want to go home yet.

"Which place do you like more?"

"I like them both for different reasons. Which place do you like more?"

"Of course, I love my home. I haven't been to America, so I don't yet know how it is, but in movies and on TV it is a good place."

"Why don't you come and stay with me for a few months so that we each will have stayed in both places and can make a better decision."

"Jurnee?"

"Anooj?"

"I married such a brilliant woman," he said as he took my hand in his. "I'm glad we got married. I'm happy to live anywhere you want to be."

"Me too," I smiled.

"Aaand," he drew out the syllable, "Since you're almost done with your dinner, I'll tell you the surprise."

I immediately dropped my fork. "*Sollunga*," I said, mustering up a tiny bit of practice Tamil to force him to tell me.

"Ooty is a little bit famous for fudge," he said as he pulled out a small box.

"When did you get this?" I asked, shocked. He had been with me the whole time.

"I snuck out while you were sleeping earlier. I knew you would want chocolates."

And he was absolutely right.

The next morning, we woke up early to get ready for the photographer. I washed my hair and put it back neatly in a half ponytail, took my new burgundy *churidar* with golden embellishments, and started to get ready when my face dropped.

"What happened?" Anooj asked, concerned.

"I forgot the *kumkum*, and we don't have jasmine." Everything was ruined.

"He can add in edits, don't think about it."

"Are you sure? Should we go buy some? I totally forgot."

"It's fine. Do you still want me to wear this dress?" he said, pointing to the blue button-up and khaki pants.

"*Aamaa*," I confirmed, practicing my Tamil, as I picked up our other two outfits so they would be ready to change easily later. My second outfit was the yellow *churidar* set, and his was the red checkered button-up. My third outfit was the red shirt with jeans, and his was the blue T-shirt with jeans. It felt excessive, but he had said to choose three.

Anooj's phone rang, and he began speaking Tamil and gesturing towards the door. The photographer must be here.

With one last look in the mirror, I followed him out the door and outside. The photographer got out and nodded to the *auto* indicating that I should get in. Anooj sat in the middle, and the photographer sat on the edge. I tried to move as close to the side as I could to make enough room, but it really wasn't meant for three adults to sit comfortably.

We drove through the main high-traffic area until it slowly became less and less crowded. We drove by a small church, and he said something to the driver that made him stop. It was a very cute little church that reminded me of the one back in Kumbalam. It was a bright beige color and had castle-like details on the roof that reminded me of the rook piece in Chess.

But we didn't go inside. He spoke to Anooj briefly as we stood beside some wildflowers on the edge of the driveway, took a few pictures, then we immediately got back into the *auto*.

"What was that about?" I whispered to Anooj. "Why didn't we go inside?"

"The color matched part of your *dupatta*, so he thought it would look good. That's all."

We continued driving into the hills. They were a bit bumpier than the ideal conditions for taking an *auto* ride, but it was gorgeous. The roads became more curved. The lush greenery became thicker. There were more monkeys. And I was terrified.

The *auto* stopped at the foot of a huge hill. There were people everywhere, but I felt a bit silly being the only ones with a private photographer. A few stared, and I wondered what they were thinking. *People stare even without a camera,* I reminded myself. *Don't be so concerned about what others are thinking about you. This is your honeymoon. Your grandchildren will see these photos. Enjoy yourself.*

No one was as good at scolding me as myself, and I shifted my focus to Anooj as we followed the photographer's directions to hold hands and stare at each other. I couldn't help but to laugh at how silly I felt staring at him, and he laughed at me laughing for no reason.

The photographer paused for a moment to look at the photos, then shouted to us, "Laugh again!"

I guess it looked okay. We continued doing various poses, both seated and standing, before rejoining the driver and moving on to the next place.

The trees became denser, and there were more and more monkeys the further we went in. *How much further will we go?* I wondered just as we approached a makeshift parking lot.

People were walking around the forest; some were having lunch and some were taking photos. A few of the women also had elaborate *marudhaani* all the way up their arms, maybe they had just gotten married, too.

We stood beside the trees in various poses until he decided that we were finished and went back to the AirBNB to change to our next outfits.

I carefully changed to my yellow *churidar*, trying to not mess up my hair and also get the *dupatta* pinned symmetrically at the same time. I far preferred stiff *dupattas* like the one with the previous *churidar* because you just put it on one shoulder and call it a day. The ones that go across both shoulders had a lot more variables to them and required a lot more dexterity to put a safety pin behind your shoulder on both sides. How could I master a *saree* if I couldn't even master a *dupatta*? I was hopeless.

A knock came on the door. "Are you ready?" Anooj asked. He had finished long before me and gone to the hall to meet the photographer.

"Almost," I said wistfully, hoping it was true.

A few minutes later, I joined them in the hall, and we went back outside to get in the *auto*. *How much was it going to cost to have an auto driver on retainer for the entire day?* But he wasn't there

"Where is he?" I whispered to Anooj. "Was he angry that I took too long? Do we need to call another?" I instantly felt guilty.

"No, he had to go home for a minute. He will come back, then we will go for lunch."

"But I don't want to get my clothes dirty."

"First we will take pictures around the property, then we will change and go to lunch."

We stood at the base of a particularly wide tree with a ladder at the base. We pushed each other on the swings. We sat at a table. We walked towards the camera. But the whole time, my stomach was audibly growling.

"Are you okay?" Anooj asked. "Should we call him to go right now?

"No, it's fine." I wouldn't *die*, I just felt so hungry. It had been nearly five hours, and it was *way* past lunch time. I could manage a bit longer.

"No, no. Come. We'll change and go." He turned to the photographer and said something in Tamil that, by tone, sounded like asking confirmation that he was finished.

The photographer nodded his head as we started to go inside, and Anooj pulled out his phone to call the driver.

Changing into a polo was much easier than a *churidar* with *dupatta*, and I finished in just a couple of minutes. By the time we got outside, the driver and photographer were outside waiting for us. It was finally time to have lunch. At three in the afternoon.

I instantly regretted my decision to stuff myself with *dosa* when American clothes were much more fitted than Indian clothes. I would be clearly bloated in the photos.

But there was nothing that I could do now, so I got back into the *auto* and took in the scenic views around me. The real India was strikingly different than the misconceptions that so many held.

Last year when I had just come home from Kerala, my first trip to India, I had been met with questions about if India smelled terrible, how dirty it was, how safe I felt. I had honestly told them my experiences and worked to prove their assumptions wrong. I felt that I owed India something for everything it had given me. I'd had such an unforgettable few months, and I didn't want anyone to have the wrong idea and potentially miss out on such an amazing place with such kind people.

The auto stopped suddenly, and we were on the edge of a beautiful garden. There were flowers *everywhere*, and I was transfixed.

We sat in the midst of wildflowers, standing side by side against a flowering hedge. We held hands in front of a peacock topiary. It was *gorgeous*, and I loved exploring another side of India. I'd lived the village life, the city life, and now I was standing at the foot of an elephant topiary in a massive garden. India had so many dimensions, and I thanked my lucky stars that I would be able to spend my life exploring them.

The next few days were much more relaxed. Exploring every restaurant, shopping for knickknacks, taking long naps, and enjoying our final few days together. After Ooty, it was back to Madurai for just a couple of days before going home. We would be separated again soon, and I wanted to soak in every second because we weren't certain when we would be able to actually start our new life together.

The train leaving Ooty was unlike anything I had ever seen before. It was unlike the Indian train I had taken, and also unlike any American train I had taken. It was small, slow, and the scenery was more picturesque than a postcard. It wasn't made for the destination, it was made for the journey.

I wanted to stay forever and not go back to real life. I wanted to stay in this green heaven with Anooj, fudge, and long naps with a fireplace.

But it wasn't realistic. The train was rather slow due to the terrain, but it felt too fast. I didn't want it to be over. I wasn't ready to go home.

From the train, we took another bus and arrived back in Madurai to spend a few more days with his family before it was time to go home.

Walking back into the house, Anooj called, "*Amma?*" and his mother came around to meet us.

Seeing that we had returned, her eyes lit up, and she quickly came to welcome us with a little pot of *kumkum*.

They spoke for a moment in Tamil before Anooj turned to me, "We're transferring your *thali* to the permanent chain today. The transfer is called *Thali Korkum.*"

I had grown to like the turmeric-stained string, but I was excited to see what would happen.

A few hours later, Devi's family and a few other relatives came to the house for the transferring. We all sat on the floor, myself in the middle.

The yellow string was removed carefully, and the knots that held the three pendants were untied. Anooj's mother went to retrieve a small bar and screw that she carefully threaded through the *thali* and pendant holes before a few of the women came to compare it with their *thalis* to be sure that it was straight. Once approved, Anooj's mother tightly screwed it to secure it in place.

With the *marudhaani* beginning to fade and the *thali* on the permanent chain, our wedding seemed long behind us. It felt like yesterday, but also like months ago.

"Now we can go to the Meenakshi Temple," Anooj said.

"What do you mean? We already went."

"But now we can go to the middle like you wanted. You're married to a Hindu now."

"Really? That's all it takes?" Would I really get to see the inside now? Telling me I can't go somewhere will really only make me want to go there even more. I wondered what was there that was so secret. It must be so beautiful and amazing if it was hidden away with limited access.

"When do you want to go?" he asked.

"Can we go now?" laughter scattered around the room at my eagerness to visit the inside of the Meenakshi Temple.

"We'll go tomorrow morning," he promised. "Before it gets too hot."

CHAPTER 16

First thing in the morning, I took a *head bath,* knowing it would be required, and put on my favorite green *churidar* with the stiff red *dupatta.*

Anooj woke up and immediately laughed that I was already ready. "Why are you so excited?" he teased me.

"Why *aren't* you excited?"

"I am from Madurai. I have gone a hundred times."

"Well I am from America, and I have only gone half of a time because I couldn't see the inside."

He laughed, "Why are you so persistent?"

"*Udaney vaanga,*" I said to practice my Tamil and tell him to come immediately.

"*Seri, ma,*" he agreed. "What do you want for breakfast?"

"We can have food at the temple, get ready fast," I demanded.

A half hour later, we were parking his motorcycle and leaving our phones with the jeweler. We gave our sandals to the shoe check-in like last time. We walked into the line like last time. But this time, we would be going into the middle.

"I'll be right back," Anooj whispered as he started to walk away.

"Where are you going?"

"To buy the ticket."

"We have to buy tickets?"

"Unless you want to stand in line for hours."

"But why can't I come?"

"Because they might not sell both tickets to me if you come. Just wait two minutes."

My heart sank. When would I be recognized as more than just a foreigner? If I moved here, would I always be made to feel like I didn't belong? What if I was 50 and had lived more than half my life here, would it still happen then?

Examining the ticket, I noticed that it was just over a dollar to skip the long line, with many choosing to save the money and wait for hours instead. The currency inequality hit me hard, and I immediately felt a pang of guilt.

After waiting about fifteen minutes in the line, it was our turn to go inside, but the guard stopped us and said something sternly to Anooj in Tamil. Anooj pointed to my *thali*, but the guard's voice remained stern.

"What happened?" I whispered as we walked out of the line.

"He said that we need to take permission from the temple superintendent."

"Seriously?"

He nodded as we walked a few yards to the empty office. There was no sign saying when someone would be back. The door was locked. There wasn't a secretary or anyone to ask how much longer it would take.

We waited about twenty minutes before Anooj grew impatient. "I'll try one more time," Anooj said as he started to walk back to the post.

"No wait, I'll try."

"He probably won't know English."

"But he'll probably know Tamil," I said, way too confident in my speaking abilities. I hadn't even been brave enough to speak my broken Tamil to my in-laws, and now I was going to try with a complete stranger. With a deep breath, I walked back to the post, practicing my sentence silently in my head so I wouldn't mess it up.

He looked at me sternly, but his face softened as I spoke. "*Anna, avanga ingae illa,*" I said, addressing him respectfully as my elder brother while telling him that the superintendent was not there.

He smiled and nodded affirmatively that I could go inside. It had worked! I quickly waved to Anooj, and the man said something to Anooj in Tamil as we went through the gate.

"What did he say?" I asked, curiously.

"That I'm very lucky. What did you say to him?"

"*Anna, avanga ingae illa,*" I repeated.

"That's all it took?" he was shocked.

"Of course. Didn't you realize that my Tamil was better than yours?"

We both laughed at the ridiculousness of my statement and finally reached the inside.

But it wasn't the inside. It was another line.

"More lines? What is this?"

"The inside of the temple," he said amused. "What were you expecting?"

"Some big sculptures and something secret. Why else would you want to keep everyone out?

"It's only non-Hindus that don't come inside," he said. "Because inside, we take blessings, and non-Hindus won't be interested in that."

I stood on my tip toes to see the front of the line and saw that there was, in fact, a man at the end with a tray of white powder he was pressing onto the foreheads of all who passed him.

After an hour, we reached the front of the line. I hated thinking how long it took for those without the fast pass. I studied the people ahead of me in line to see what they were doing. It seemed that they all pressed their palms together and slightly tilted their heads toward him.

I decided to do a practice run when we were about ten people away from the front.

"What are you doing?" Anooj asked.

"I wanted to practice."

"Practice for what?"

"I don't want to do it wrong," I admitted nervously. "What if I mess up and he gets angry?"

He laughed gently, "You can't do it wrong. Don't worry so much."

When it was finally our turn, the priest looked at me, surprised, then applied the ash as I closed my eyes and pressed my palms together as I had practiced. I did it!

We went to the second line, which gave *kumkum*, and the priest at that station applied it over the ash. I had officially completed my visit to the inner sanctum of the Meenakshi Temple. This was the greatest moment of my life.

Leaving the inner area, we were each given *prasadam*, the food that had been blessed. I was starving, and it was a perfect spherical oily delicious *ladoo*.

After ordering more, we went to sit outside like we had the time before. But this time was different. Everyone stared at me, but after noticing my *thali* and toe rings, they looked away. Like I had overcome their scrutiny. I belonged here now.

When we got home, Anooj told everyone the story in Tamil, and they laughed heartily and smiled at me approvingly. I had a long way to go, but I was starting to fit in.

"We'll go for movie?" Aarthi asked as she ran to my side.

"Sure, which?" That sounded like so much fun! I hadn't been to a theater in India before.

"Dhanush is having new movie!" she exclaimed.

Dhanush was one of my favorite actors, and I really wanted to go, but I was almost certain that they wouldn't have subtitles.

"Do they have subtitles?" I asked, cautiously optimistic.

"Don't want. You are knowing Tamil now," she said confidently.

Oh, how I wished knowing Tamil was that easy, but I smiled to agree, and they immediately started making the plan.

After a few minutes of Tamil discussions, I asked Anooj, "So, what's happening?"

"We're going to buy the tickets online, and after the movie, we are deciding which restaurant to go to for your last night."

I had almost forgotten for a moment that this was the last night. I remembered the first time I had been at the airport leaving and how happy and dressed up everyone else was, like I was the only one who had ever dreaded leaving India. I wasn't ready to go home yet. To go to my other home? This was my home now, too, wasn't it? Married life was confusing. Especially when it spanned two continents.

The theater was much different than I had expected. I'd been expecting it to be similar to American theaters, but it was so much *better*.

There was security when going inside. The seats were assigned and only a couple of dollars each. Popcorn wasn't ten dollars. They even had ice cream! Serving sizes were painfully small, though. The interior was gorgeous, and I'd never seen a theater so fancy.

"Are all theaters in India like this?" I asked Anooj.

"Some are, we have simple ones, too. We just wanted you to have the fancy experience."

I chuckled to myself, diva foreigner strikes again.

The movie itself was good, as are all Dhanush movies. He often takes socially responsible roles that give good messages on ways to improve society. Some of his movies are fun flicks, but most are quite meaningful, and he had come to be one of my favorite Tamil actors.

After the movie, we went to the famed Madurai Paati Kadai. It was a beautiful restaurant with a woman sitting at the front. It was her restaurant, and she was the *paati* for whom it was named.

Her eyes lit up when she saw us arrive, and she immediately called me to sit beside her. I looked up at her, the idyllic Tamil grandma. Her ear lobes hung, stretched from years of heavy ornate earrings. Her grey hair tied back in a tight bun that mysteriously held without any instruments. Her eyes were both warm and wise, and it felt like she was looking into my soul.

"Where is your child?" she asked me.

"I don't have one," I responded shyly. We had only just gotten married; it didn't happen that quickly.

Devi began speaking to her in Tamil, and *Paati* took my hand in hers as she traced the fading *marudhaani*.

"On your next trip to India, you will come to me with a baby." I wasn't sure if it was a prediction, a request, or a demand, but I smiled as she told me about the old days in perfect English. If it was a prediction, I hoped it wouldn't be as accurate as my magic husband leaf had been. We still had plenty of time.

She was a brilliant storyteller, and we sat silently listening to her tell us about her life, her children, her restaurant... until a man came suddenly and said something in Tamil that made everyone laugh.

I looked to Anooj, hoping to be filled in on the joke as everyone stood up and went inside.

"He was telling her that we came to eat so we must be hungry."

"But she is so nice."

"But we're also hungry."

I guess it was technically true.

Everyone had non-veg except for me. I ordered another *dosa* and ate it sadly, not knowing when I would have my next.

Tomorrow, I would be leaving India for the third time. It felt like I had two lives. In one life, I was a teacher, a friend, a daughter. I lived at home, and I had a good job. Most of my time was spend independently doing what I wanted to do, and there were rigid boundaries and rules.

But in my life in India, everything was different. Everything intersected, and there were no boundaries. Time went by more slowly, and people really listened when you spoke. I felt more at home and welcomed in India than I had ever felt at home.

Family here was different than it was back home. Family here was barely going a day without seeing each other, and the lines blurred between immediate family and extended family. Family here was showing up, not making appointments. Family here was dropping everything if someone said they needed something, not referring them to another person.

For me, reverse culture shock had always been more severe than the initial culture shock.

The next day, I woke up dreading my flight that night. Soon, I would be away from Anooj and his family, and back home listening to excuses about why people didn't come for the wedding. At least I had a couple of months of vacation until school started again.

"Do you want to wash your clothes before you go home, or do you want to wait until you're home?" Anooj asked.

"Depends. Do I have to do it by hand?" I had learned how to at the hostel, but I preferred not to. At least I didn't have any jeans to wash, those had been absolutely dreadful to wash by hand.

"No, we have a machine. Bring your clothes, I'll show you."

I gathered them all in my arms and followed him out the door and through the kitchen into a small room just before the back door. There sat a washing machine that looked normal by all standards, but it was slightly smaller.

I put everything inside and added a little bit of detergent before closing the lid and starting the load.

But nothing happened.

"Did I break it?" I asked Anooj.

"No," he laughed. "You didn't turn it on." He flipped the switch on the wall connected to the outlet. I was always forgetting to turn on outlet switches and grimaced at my mistake.

The little green lights immediately came on, and I began to read the options. They all seemed the same as home, with one exception. There was a setting specifically for *sarees*. Amazing. If only washers back home had that setting. Dry cleaning was going to be expensive.

After the washing had finished, Anooj helped me hang up the clothes in the backyard, and his mother came behind us to surprise us with fresh guava.

I didn't like the guava at home from the store, but fresh guava was delicious. I silently added it to my infinite list of things I would miss about India.

When we got back inside, Devi's family had come.

Aarthi ran to me and said, "*Aththai,* when will you come back?"

"Hopefully soon," I replied sullenly.

"Then don't want to go."

I smiled. I didn't, but I also didn't want to make a scene or risk crying. "I'll come soon," I promised.

"Then what will you do at your home?" Devi asked.

"Right now is summer break, so I will return to school in August."

She looked shocked. "Then why are you going? Stay here some more time."

I wished that I could. I should have. But it was too late now. Flights were extremely expensive to change as I had learned the first time I came. I felt a tear beginning to form and quickly looked away.

"Did you pack your things? Is there anything you need to buy before going?" she asked.

Anooj suddenly interjected. "Do you want some *Mysore Pak* before going?"

I had totally forgotten. "Yes! Thank you for reminding me."

"We should go soon so you have enough time."

"Go now," Devi said with a nod.

And with that, we took his motorcycle back to my favorite Sri Krishna Sweets. The familiar blue signage. The long counter with endless snacks, both sweet and spicy.

"*Mysore Pak* sample," Anooj requested as he handed us two tiny slices.

It melted perfectly, and I wanted to eat it every day for the rest of my life.

"Three *kg*," he ordered. It always caught me off guard when he said *kg* instead of *kilogram*, but I watched patiently as the man packaged it up for us. "And half *kg* also," he finished.

"For your family?"

He nodded to confirm as we paid and walked outside. Watching the sun began to set, I realized that this would be my last Indian sunset for who knew how long.

"I'll miss you, Jurnee," he said as we got back on his motorcycle.

"I don't want to go home," I admitted.

"Then what will I do with my flight ticket?"

"Your what?"

"My flight to America."

"But you don't have a visa yet."

"Yes, I do," he winked.

"How?"

"I applied for one."

"Ha. Ha," It wasn't funny.

"I'm serious. I applied secretly because I didn't know how long it will take. I'm coming after a month."

A single shocked tear immediately fell, and I hugged him way too tightly in the middle of a crowded street. Luckily, I was already sitting behind him on his motorcycle with my hand on him for balance, so it didn't look too out of place. He was really coming.

"How long will you stay for?"

"Three months."

"How did you get that much time off?"

"Are you happy I'm coming or not?" he teased. "What is this interrogation?"

"Okay, okay, fine. But really, how? Do you still have a job? You took off so much time for the wedding and then three months? How is it possible?"

"My project is finishing soon, so I asked for a gap between projects."

I guess that made sense.

"We have to make one more stop," he said as we started to go near the temple again.

"We're going to the temple?"

"No, the jeweler."

"Is everything fine?"

"We have to buy a ring."

"What for? I have two and you have one."

"Not for us."

"Then?"

"For my sister and her husband, for doing so much for the wedding."

He then explained all the work they had done with every aspect of the wedding. They had planned, organized, managed vendors, and even spent some of their own money. I hadn't realized how much work it had taken to pull everything off, and they worked tirelessly to make sure we had a good wedding, without expecting anything in return.

We went inside the small shop and looked at a few rings before Anooj selected one and began to stand as the owner packaged it.

"What about your sister? You said both of them."

"This is for both of them."

"But they can't both wear it."

"Neither will wear it. It is just to gift gold."

"We should get for her also," I insisted.

Anooj spoke to the owner and pulled out some feminine rings.

"I don't know her size. Get her earrings."

He smiled as the owner began to put the tray of feminine rings away and pull a tray of earrings. Each one had a number attached by a small tag. 2.356, 3.514, 1.836, 2.942.

"What currency is this?" I asked.

"It's not currency. It's the weight of the gold."

Ohh. That made more sense. I looked through the different styles and settled on one that had three long gold strands hanging from the base, each with a red stone. It was beautiful, and she had a lot of *sarees* that it would match.

"This one?" Anooj had caught me staring at it.

I nodded, and the jeweler packed it also as Anooj stood to leave.

"Shouldn't we pay?" I asked.

"He is a family friend. We don't pay every time. We will settle the account later."

The owner looked confused and nodded to Anooj, silently asking if everything was fine. He replied in Tamil, and the owner began laughing and nodded that it was fine for us to go.

I waved as we went outside, now almost dark.

When we got back to the house, we presented the boxes to Devi and Naren as they looked up at us, confused.

Anooj said something in Tamil, and they began to open them. Naren seemed to be saying there was no need to buy anything for them, but Devi was thrilled. She immediately took out her earrings to put in the new ones. It was such a relief that she liked them.

I went out back to take my clothes from the lines but found them already folded and smiled. They actually liked me. Just a few months ago we were terrified, but we had had nothing to be afraid of. Everything was perfect.

"Are you ready?" Anooj asked as he came behind me. "We should go soon."

I nodded unenthusiastically.

"I'll be there soon. Then you can show me America," he smiled.

"Not soon enough," I shrugged.

He helped me put the last of my things in the suitcase, then hugged me tightly. "Even if I am not with you, I am always with you," he assured me.

"I know," I breathed deeply, careful to not cry.

"Ready?" he asked.

"No."

"I'm being serious."

"So am I."

"One month. Just one month. I'll be there before you know it."

"Why can't you come sooner? Come now."

"Tickets are really expensive if you don't buy them a month or two in advance," he sighed. He wanted to come sooner, too.

With a final hug, unsure if someone would come through the door, he picked up my suitcase and started towards the door. I picked up my backpack and followed him.

We said our goodbyes to the family, and I leaned my head down while his mother pressed my forehead with something wet and slightly cold. I smiled and waved to them, not wanting to prolong the goodbye in an effort to avoid crying in front of them.

In the car, I stopped caring and started crying.

"Always crying. What is this?" he teased me.

I wasn't in a mood to be teased and looked at him angrily.

"Okay, okay," he retracted. "Just one more month okay, don't think so much."

"But I want to be here," I admitted.

"In India?"

I nodded.

"But everyone in India is dying to go to America."

"You are all wrong," I sighed.

He laughed. "You are very backwards."

"Maybe *you're* backwards, and I'm frontwards," I retorted.

We both started laughing until we saw the airport just ahead.

CHAPTER 17

Coming home married but being alone was surreal, in the worst way possible. My life was exactly the same, and it felt like nothing had happened, like it had all been my imagination. Had it all been a dream? I shut myself in my room, away from everyone and everything that reminded me I was no longer in India.

I still lived at home. I still lived without Anooj. I was lonely, but I was still hurt by no one coming and didn't want to meet them yet. Looking at the calendar, I counted the days until Anooj would arrive. Twenty more sleeps.

I was jetlagged, and with school being closed for the summer and having no motivation to go anywhere, I felt like it was going to last forever. It was the middle of the night, and I had just woken up.

Are you awake? I texted him out of habit, even though he should definitely be awake.

Obviously, he replied with a laughing emoji. *What are you doing?*

Sethruvaen, I replied. My new favorite phrase to indicate that I would die soon.

You can't always say this, he scolded.

I will.

Are you busy? Should I call or is it too late?

I don't want to wake up my parents, I sent reluctantly. He was my husband, and I couldn›t even speak to him.

Come to Skype, we will silently call and chat.

I wiped the few tears that had fallen out and answered the video. There he sat, absolutely perfect except for being ten thousand miles away.

Do you want to watch a movie together? he typed.

Which one?

Do you want English or Tamil?

Anything is fine. It wasn't like I would be able to focus anyway.

Tell me a movie you liked when you were a kid. We'll see that.

I tried to think of a movie that he would like. *Clueless? What's it about?*

Quintessential 90s movie about a rich girl in California.

I could see him typing and erasing. He thought it sounded terrible.

It's better than it sounds, I replied quickly.

Ok sure. Netflix?

Yep, I replied as I started to open my browser.

Sooooo, I asked after it finished.

It wasn't too bad, he admitted.

Ha. You loved it. Don't lie.

Only because Mike Hannigan was in it.

Who?

On Friends.

You're such a nerd, I teased.

Are you tired? Or hungry?

A little hungry, but not tired.

We'll eat together. Go and bring some snacks.

I wished more than anything that he was here. Or that I was there. This was absolute torture, but I went downstairs. Something was better than nothing. At least we were married.

Going downstairs to the old familiar kitchen, I couldn't help but to get flashbacks of the kitchen in India. The gas stovetop. The water filter. The scratchy metal sponge. The huge jars of spices. I missed everything and reached into the cupboard to pull out of a box of cookies. But they weren't Dark Fantasy. They weren't Hide and Seek. They weren't even Good Day.

With a glass of water and my box of cookies, I hurried back upstairs to meet Anooj.

Biscuits? he teased.

I rolled my eyes and started eating them. I didn't care if it was gluttonous. I was sad and wanted cookies.

I miss you, Jurnee, he sent.

I miss you more. I felt like a lovestruck teenager talking like that and started to laugh.

What happened?

Come now, I demanded.

Just a few more days. I'll be there soon.

What do you want to do when you come?

You stay near Chicago, right?

Ya.

Then we'll go for Chicago.

For three months? There was way more to do than just go to Chicago.

Niagara Falls?

Sure. What else?

Grand Canyon?

Make a list and we'll plan a big road trip.

Road trip means the long car journeys in Hollywood movies?

Ya.

Ok, then we will see everything. Do you have enough time?

I'm free until the end of July.

So, I will take one month journey with Jurnee then we will spend two months at home.

Sounds perfect.

AnooJurnee will take a new journey.

I had totally forgotten his name pun he created when he'd asked me out last year and smiled. As much as I hated puns and corny cringey things, I loved him more than anything.

I rolled my eyes and smiled; this was who I was going to spend the rest of my life with. I had gotten so lucky.

Not getting sleepy? he asked.

Light was beginning to peek through the curtains. It would be morning soon. *Na. I think I'll try to stay awake all day so maybe I can sleep tonight. It's been so hard to adjust this time.*

Don't make yourself tense. Sleep anytime, your body will naturally find its rhythm again. Don't worry.

He was right. He always was. *I think I'll try to sleep so I can stay awake longer tonight.*

Ok da. Call when you wake up. If you want.

Of course, I want to, loosu. *You're my husband.*
Didn't you know that every wife hates her husband?
Ok fine, I'll try to like you less.
But not too less.

Goodnight, yennenga, I sent, using the traditional pet
name Tamil wives used for their husbands.

He sent the emoji with hearts in its eyes, and I closed
my eyes, begging sleep to come to me.

I groggily rolled over and looked at my phone. It was just
past ten, and I was late for my Tamil class. It hadn't even
occurred to me to set an alarm. I hadn't anticipated it
taking that long.

Logging in to my Tamil class website, I waved to my
teacher apologetically. "Sorry!"

"It's okay. Slept well?"

"No. I have the worst jetlag."

"*Paaravaala,*" he said, telling me it was no problem.
"We will take it easy today, then."

He began reviewing some simple sentences, and I
slowly started waking up. He was very good at reading
me and knew exactly when I was losing focus and needed
a break, or when it was getting too tough and I needed
to slow down. I felt so lucky to have found such a great
Tamil teacher. The hour passed by quickly.

"You'll be fluent within a year if you keep trying,"
he promised.

"*Apdiya?*" I replied, asking if it was really so.

"*Kandippa,*" he said confidently, and I hoped he was right.

"*Seri, paakalaam,*" I said, effectively ending the call by telling him we'd see each other later.

"*Paakalaam,*" he confirmed.

Feeling confident in my speaking, I decided to try to call Anooj's mom and try to speak.

It rang once, and my heart started racing. Twice and I could feel my palms beginning to sweat. On the third ring, she answered.

"Hello?"

"*Eppadi irukkeenga?*" I said, asking how she was.

She laughed, "*Nalla irukkaen,*" she replied, indicating that she was well, before she started speaking far above my vocabulary level.

"*Enna?*" I asked.

She repeated something that I didn't understand.

"*Theriyala,*" I replied, telling her that I didn't know. She laughed nervously.

"*Ennoda Thamizh romba mosamaana,*" I admitted my Tamil was truly awful. I had overestimated my fluency.

"*Illa!*" she rejected my statement before beginning to speak quickly again.

I tried to reply, but my words were jumbled. "*Eh?*" she asked, having as much of a difficult time understanding me as I had had understanding her. I promised myself that I would work harder on my Tamil.

"*Saapaadula vengaayam mathiri ennoda thappu paesum pozhuthu,*" I said, attempting my first complex sentence and hoping that it made sense. I had told her that my mistakes while speaking were as common as onions in food, a bad attempt at a joke in a language I could barely speak.

She paused for a moment then began laughing heartily. She had understood my joke. We were bonding. *One day, we might even be able to have an actual conversation*, I hoped.

That afternoon, I had planned to make *dosa* and chutney for my parents to expose them a little bit to Tamil Nadu.

"So, what is this again?" my dad asked as I took the white tub of Priyem's premade batter out of the refrigerator.

"It's like a really thin fried pancake with tomato sauce."

"Pancakes and ketchup?" my mom looked confused.

I rolled my eyes, "Just try it, dad."

"We're just teasing you, pumpkin," he said with a laugh.

I dropped a spoonful of batter on the hot skillet and began spreading it outwards clockwise. Drizzling a bit of oil around the edges, I waited for the batter to bubble up, then flipped it to reveal a golden-brown underneath. I had made a *dosa*. Luckily, I'd already made the chutney the night before, so it just needed to be heated up.

After a few more *dosas* had been made, I set them out with a heavy dollop of chutney and carefully watched my parents' reactions.

They dipped it like tortilla chips, just as I had back in Kerala on my first trip. I had purposely made it not spicy so it should be okay, but my fingers were quietly crossed behind my back. *Please like it, please like it.*

My dad looked up with a smile. "That's great!"

"So, this is what they eat in India? What about the *chicken tikka masala*?" she asked.

"They have more than one dish, Mom. There are literally billions of people." *You would know that if you had come*, I said silently. I had been trying hard to not hold a grudge about them not coming, but it was hard.

"Make a few more," she said.

"You're still hungry?"

"No, Krista and Marina are coming."

My heart sank into my stomach. I really didn't want to see them.

"We know you're upset, but you can't hold it against everyone forever."

I definitely could. But the doorbell rang. Shit.

"Come in!" my mom shouted as I flipped another *dosa.*

They walked in timidly, holding a bag. I didn't want any gifts. My parents took the cue and dismissed themselves to the living room.

"You came for *dosa*?" I asked them.

"We miss you, Jurnee," Krista started.

"And we brought you a wedding gift!" Marina added.

" I don't want a gift. I wanted you to be there." I felt bad being upset, but it had been really important to me. How could they not be there for me during such an important time in my life?

"We're sorry, Jurnee."

"Truly. We made a huge mistake, and we're so sorry for hurting you. We didn't mean to. We didn't think it through, and we would be devastated if you didn't come to our weddings."

"And we missed out on such a great opportunity to see India. Your pictures were gorgeous. When we watched the livestream and saw you alone, we felt so awful."

"What livestream?"

"Anooj messaged everyone the day before your wedding. He set it up with the photographer so that we could all be there."

Had he really? Why didn't he tell me? He was always trying to do every little thing to make me more comfortable or happier. How had I gotten so lucky? I half smiled. I *had* missed them, and it would really suck to hold a grudge against them forever. "Fine," I said reluctantly.

"You don't hate us anymore?" Krista asked hopefully.

"We love you, Jurnee. We're the absolute worst," Marina admitted as she pulled the two of us into a group hug.

"I love you guys, too."

"So, do you want your present now?"

"You guys really didn't need to get me anything."

"Yes, we did! You're the first of us to get married!"

Marina handed me the bag excitedly, and I opened it slowly, unsure of what to expect.

It was a wood cutout in Tamil letters. I couldn't read Tamil yet, but there were tons of little pictures of Anooj and I spread out on the wood.

"What does it say?" I asked them.

"The Etsy guy said it means *love*," Marina said as she checked her phone. "Wait, no, it's *coddle*. Does that mean *love?*" she asked with the most horrendous mispronunciation I'd ever heard.

"It's pronounced *kaa-dhull,*" I corrected her with a laugh. I had corrected someone's Tamil; I really was getting better.

"Do you like it?" Krista asked eagerly.

"I love it."

"You mean you *kaadhal* it? Marina joked as I rolled my eyes. "When are we going to meet him?"

"You could have met him already if you'd come for the wedding," I said pointedly. Perhaps too pointedly.

"Burn," Krista chipped in like it was 2003 again.

"He's coming in a few weeks, actually."

"Really? That's great! For how long?"

"Three months."

Suddenly, it hit me. Anooj wasn't just going to be seeing America and trying real tacos for the first time. He was going to meet my family and friends and see how I live. I was realizing how huge this was and started getting nervous. What if he didn't like it here? What if it changed his perception of me and he stopped liking *me?*

"What happened?" Marina asked.

"Just nervous."

"Why?"

"What if he doesn't like me anymore once he comes here?"

Krista laughed. "You're literally married. He's legally obligated to like you."

Marina and I looked at each other and couldn't stop laughing.

"What? It's true!"

And just like that, everything went back to normal. Though I still felt hurt, it was important to realize that no one is perfect and that holding a grudge would only serve to hurt me. I was still hopeful that one day I'd convince them to visit India with me. They *had* to see what they were missing out on.

On a warm July afternoon, it was finally time to make the two-and-a-half-hour drive to Chicago to pick up Anooj. It was sunny and bright outside, the perfect day for someone to come see America for the first time. I wanted to show him everything, and I couldn't wait to see him again.

Frantically navigating the complex parking at O'Hare Arrivals, I noticed the message on my phone.

On the way out. I got my bag, he sent.

I immediately parked and ran the whole way from the parking lot to the lobby, spotting him as he walked out of the baggage claim area. Somehow, he still looked amazing after travelling twenty-six hours straight. How was it possible?

Making eye contact, we ran to each other like in the movies and hugged each other tightly. He was finally here.

Thank you for reading *The Marriage.*

Author's Note

Back in early 2017, I met Kannan at an event in Illinois hosted by a mutual friend. Both of us being introverts, we found ourselves at the edge of the room where he started some small talk. He randomly asked me, "What is your favorite Indian food?" And me, having been to India six times, asked him to clarify whether I should choose a northern or southern dish.

Shocked that I knew the difference, we became fast friends. We were engaged in November 2018 and married in May 2019. Though Kannan's backstory as Anooj has many differences, the events that unfolded around our wedding are largely similar.

Any intercultural relationship, especially around the wedding, will have some difficulties, but I consider myself truly lucky to have married Kannan and to have married into his incredible family. I hope you enjoy reading about our experience and would love to hear about yours on social media.

Quora.com/Samantha-kannan
Twitter.com/NaanSamantha
Instagram.com/SamanthaKannan
TikTok.com/@SamanthaKannan

Above: Kannan's sister trying to help me relax as we waited for the reception to begin.

Below: Admiring a giant tree on our honeymoon in Ooty.

Above: Kannan tying the *thali* around my neck to symbolize the completion of the wedding.

Below: Our wedding band.

Above: Kannan's friends expressing shock at the giant 10kg cake we had ordered

Below: Meeting my students Rukmini and Jasmine from Kerala who travelled to Madurai with their father.

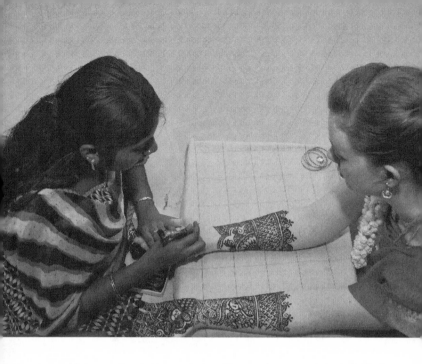

Above: Getting my *marudhaani* done two days before the wedding.

Right: Posing with Kannan after the wedding was finished.

Made in the USA
Columbia, SC
01 June 2023

17598795R00169